영어 회화의 결정적 단어들

圖解英語會話
關鍵單字

陳靖婷——譯

徐寧助——著

音檔
使用說明

STEP ❶

掃描上方 QRCode

STEP ❷

快速註冊或登入 EZCourse

STEP ❸

回答問題按送出

答案就在書中（需注意空格與大小寫）。

STEP ❹

完成訂閱

該書右側會顯示「**已訂閱**」，表示已成功訂閱，即可點選播放本書音檔。

STEP ❺

點選個人檔案

查看「**我的訂閱紀錄**」會顯示已訂閱本書，點選封面可到本書線上聆聽。

「我吃完晚餐後，會滑滑手機看訊息。」這句話的英文該如何表達？又或者「好久沒用吸塵器打掃了。」這句呢？這些日常的句子沒有任何艱澀字詞，但要用英文表達時，可能一時之間想不到適合的單字或句子。《圖解英語會話關鍵單字》就是為了這樣的人而誕生的一本書。

會話的基本是單字？

大家都說會話的基本是單字，那是因為單字組合起來會變成句子，句子的意義，也正是透過單字傳達。舉例來說，要用英文表達「我是單眼皮。」這句話，必須先知道「單眼皮」這個英文單字。若要說「我付現金。」這句話，也必須先知道「現金」這個英文單字。由此可知，想要正確溝通表達，必須先知道對應的英文單字。

一定要知道日常生活的高頻單字

既然如此，要知道怎樣的單字？又該知道多少單字呢？牛津英語辭典收錄了三十多萬個單字，我們沒辦法學這麼多單字，也沒有必要這麼做。對於非英文母語者、非口譯人員的我們來說，只要知道自己需要的單字就可以了。在日常會話中，沒有必要了解像 metaphysical（形而上學的）、subconscious（潛意識的）這樣的單字，只要知道能夠描述自己的日常生活、興趣休閒和周遭發生事情的單字就十分足夠了。

片語比單獨的單字更重要

然而必須要知道的是，並不是知道很多單字就能練就自然流暢的會話。我們講話時並非使用單獨的單字，而是將單字連結成片語、句子。舉例來說，想要說「搭地鐵」，如果只知道「subway」這個單字是不行的，必須要知道「搭地鐵」如何表達，也就是「take the subway」。若要說「我下載了那間銀行的應用程式」，也不能只知道「app」，必須要知道「下載應用程式」是「install an app」。

因為這個緣故，本書中不僅只介紹單字，而是介紹包含單字的片語表達，幫助各位能立刻運用於會話中。

務必清楚適用現代的單字和慣用語

現代人使用手機多過傳統家用電話，網路購物和海外直購也再稀鬆平常不過。為符合這樣的時代變化，書中介紹了最新的單字和片詰。除了日常生活、食衣住行、工作、健康管理等，也有網路購物、海外直購、手機、社群媒體、性別平等和社會福利等各種社會問題、環境問題，網羅了21世紀日常最常分享的各種主題與表達。

學完整本書，也許還無法達成母語人士的程度，但若能將書中內容內化成自己的，往後遇到外國人，你將不再害怕，並且能愉悅、自在地進行內容豐富的對話。各位的英文學習之路，有我為你們加油打氣！

等待春天
徐寧助 서영조

只要單字說得好，就能夠溝通！

以下 A 和 B 兩位學生都很想學好會話，為了提升實力，他們正在努力學習基本單字。一起來看看他們用什麼樣的方式學習吧！

A 我覺得會話的基本是單字，因此我主要專注學習能用在會話的單字，尤其是能用於日常會話的單字，而非學術性、哲學性的單字。此外，我不僅只是學單字，我會整個會話句一起記憶。這麼學習以後，每當有機會和外國人對話，我都能講出適當的單字和自然流暢的句子，溝通表達對我來說變簡單了。現在的我，漸漸有自信說英文了。

B 我維持學生時期的習慣，持續學習單字，每天都背誦30個新單字。我學習的方式是將英文單字和解釋一對一記憶。照理來說，這麼學習下來，一年可以記住一萬個單字，但實際上，睡一覺後大約只記得5個。此外，既然背誦已經很辛苦了，所以我將時間集中在學習艱澀單字，不過這些單字遇到外國人時幾乎用不上。因為這個因素，雖然我努力學習，會話實力卻沒有提升。

各位是如何學習的呢？雖然想要提升會話能力而學單字，但卻學習會話中絕對用不到的單字，對嗎？想要學好會話，必須要能好好傳達自己的想法和周遭狀況，想要好好傳達自己的想法和周遭狀況，就必須從身邊的事物開始學英文。重要的是如何以英文表達身邊的事物，但大部分的人卻無法跳脫學生時代的英文考試學習方式。

如果你想要學好英語會話，不妨從學單字開始嘗試。試著想想，你和母語人士討論深度哲學的機會多，還是談論日常生活和興趣休閒的機會多呢？當然是後者吧！既然如此，從現在開始就改變學單字的方式吧。如果希望快速學習單字，不用學習整個句子，只要學會說適當的單字和片語，就能達成溝通了。你也想要好好學習單字吧？那麼你應該明白，為什麼要挑選《圖解英語會話關鍵單字》這本書。

必讀《圖解英語會話關鍵單字》的關鍵原因！

1 無比豐富的主題！

　　如同前面所說，我們和外國人談論的大都是我們的日常生活和興趣休閒，但日常生活和興趣休閒的範圍其實無窮無盡。因此，這本書將談論的主題分為16大章節，再細分為數個小主題，多至11個，少至2個，平均每章節有5個小主題，並分別介紹每個主題一定要知道的單字和片語。除此之外，書中也會介紹生活上、社會上的最新單字。

2 這些片語超好用！

　　學習單字最不好的方式就是「單字－中文意思」這樣的記憶法。當然，有些單字這樣記憶也無妨，但本書不會獨立介紹單字，而是一同介紹包含單字的片語 (phrase)。獨立的單字並沒有辦法成為語言，舉例來說，若要說「擤鼻涕」，不能只知道「鼻子 (nose)」，必須知道「擤鼻涕 (blow one's nose)」這個慣用說法。若要說「趴卜！」，必須要知道「趴」為「lie on one's stomach」。書中將單字搭配慣用片語一起介紹，能幫助運用於會話之中。

3 搭配生動的圖像！

　　人類的大腦相較於僅只接收文字的方式，同時接收圖片和文字的記憶效果更為強大。書中運用這樣的優勢，同時提供圖片，幫助單字和片語的記憶效果最大化。圖像搭配單字，更容易在腦中留下鮮明的印象。此外，圖像也能讓學習更有趣、更不枯燥。

4 這些會話句超實用！

　　工欲善其事，必先利其器，單字和片語必須結合成句子，才能發揮效用。書中收錄各種口語例句，看完你會驚覺「原來這句要這麼說！」、「原來可以這麼表達！」、「我可以這麼說啊！」。

　　這麼豐富的好書，該如何使用效果最好呢？

CASE 1

給認為「書就是要從最前面開始閱讀」的你！

認為書一定要從最前面開始閱讀的你，若不這麼做，就會覺得自己錯過什麼，抑或心裡不安，對吧？這並沒有錯，也沒什麼不好。書中從自己的生活開始，逐漸拓展到自己的周遭、社會與國家，非常適合想要依序學習的人。

打開書本，左頁、右頁上方有與該主題相關以及母語人士常用的單字、片語和插圖。即使你的眼睛習慣先看英文，也請故意先看中文，並思考英文要如何説。這樣思考英文單字的過程對學單字來説非常重要。看過單字和片語以後，可以掃描 QR Code，確認單字如何發音。

2

接著，請讀左頁或右頁下方的 SENTENCES TO USE。這裡同樣請先看中文，思考英文要如何表達，接著再確認句子。這麼做你會發現，雖然是簡單的句子，但若要用英文表達，有時候並不會立刻聯想。書中收錄的句子十分口語，實用度相當高，可以在適當的時機運用。同樣地，掃描 QR Code，可以確認母語人士如何發音。注意，別只用聽的！聽完請跟著母語人士唸，多唸幾次更好，如果可以的話，背誦起來效果更佳。

書中標記說明

[   ] 表示可以取代前面的單字。
例 send[transfer] money（匯款）有 send money、transfer money 兩種説法。
(   ) 表示可以一起讀其中的單字。
例 all day (long)（一整天）表示可以説成 all day 或 all day long。
另外，像 ICU (intensive care unit) 縮寫後方的括弧，用來説明原本非縮寫的單字。

CASE 2

給認為「書為何要從最前面開始閱讀？」的你！

書一定要從最前面開始閱讀嗎？如果不是一定要讀前面內容才能明白後面內容的書，就能從任何想讀的地方開始。尤其像這樣的單字書更是如此，不妨從自己感興趣、認為有趣的地方開始。但若要用這種方式，也請遵守下面的步驟。

即使是自己知道的單字，如果發音不正確，母語人士就會聽不懂，因此正確發音也十分重要。

1

3

右頁下方（有時候在左頁下方）會整理出意思相近但用法不同的單字、一般人常誤用的表達，或上面單字的衍生用法。英文中有許多發音相近的單字，要像母語人士一樣精準掌握並不容易，為避免產生不必要的誤會，書中整理了一定要知道的注意事項。

/ 表示後方為共同單字，必須一起讀。

例 the first / second / third / only child 分別表示 the first child（老大）、the second child（老二）、the third child（老三）、the only child（獨生子女）。

此外，/ 也扮演區別詞組的角色。例 lightning 閃電 / thunder 打雷。

CHAPTER 8 休閒與興趣 Leisure & Hobbies

CHAPTER 9 工作與經濟 Jobs & Economy

CHAPTER 10 購物 Shopping

CHAPTER 11 國家 Nation

CHAPTER

1

一定要知道的表達

_____

Words & Phrases
You Must Know

was born in
出生於

age
年紀

**birthdate,
date of birth**
出生日期

birthday
生日

**Chinese zodiac
sign** 生肖

the Year of the Rat /
Ox / Tiger / Rabbit /
Dragon / Snake /
Horse / Sheep /
Monkey /
Rooster[Chicken] /
Dog / Pig

鼠 / 牛 / 虎 / 兔 / 龍 / 蛇 /
馬 / 羊 / 猴 / 雞 / 狗 / 豬年

**family
members**
家庭成員

**family
background**
家庭背景

**the first
/ second
/ third
/ only child**
（兄弟姊妹中）
老大 / 老二 / 老三
/ 獨生子女

zodiac sign 星座

Capricorn / Aquarius /
Pisces / Aries / Taurus /
Gemini / Cancer / Leo /
Virgo / Libra / Scorpio /
Sagittarius

摩羯座 / 水瓶座 / 雙魚座 /
牡羊座 / 金牛座 / 雙子座 /
巨蟹座 / 獅子座 / 處女座 /
天秤座 / 天蠍座 / 射手座

SENTENCES TO USE

我1987年出生於全州。	I was born in 1987 in the city of Jeonju.
我屬狗。	I was born in the year of the dog.
我在家中三個孩子中排行老二。	I am the second (child) of three children.
我在小型生技公司工作。	I work for a small biotech company.
我的血型是RH+ O。	My blood type is RH+ O.
我未婚。	I am single.

nationality
國籍

hometown
家鄉

gender
性別

male
男性

female
女性

**job,
occupation**
職業

**do for
a living**
做～工作

**work
for[at, in]**
在～工作

work as
從事～

blood type
血型

height
身高

weight
體重

**marital
status**
婚姻狀態

married
已婚

single
單身

表達國籍
國籍以 Korean, Chinese, French, Indian 等形容詞來表達。
My nationality is Korean. (= I am Korean.) 我的國籍是韓國。（= 我是韓國人。）

詢問職業
一般詢問職業的慣用表達是「**What do you do for a living?**」回答時可以說「**I am ~, I work for[at, in] ~, I work as ~**」。

表達宗教
要表達「我的宗教是～」時，一般會用「**I am a Catholic.**」，以表示該宗教信徒的名詞說明。除此之外，也可以說「**I am Catholic.**」，以表達宗教的形容詞回答，兩者的意思相同。

Christian 基督教徒（的） **Catholic** 天主教徒（的） **Protestant** 新教徒（的）
Buddhist 佛教徒（的） **Won Buddhist** 韓國圓佛教徒（的） **Muslim** 伊斯蘭教徒（的）

17

一天中的時刻

in the morning / afternoon / evening 在早上 / 下午 / 傍晚
at dawn 破曉時　**at sunrise** 日出時
at sunset 日落時 **at night** 在晚上
at noon[**midday**] 在中午（正午）
at midnight 在半夜（晚上12點）
all day (**long**) 一整天

頻率表達

always 總是 – **usually** 通常 – **often** 經常 – **sometimes, occasionally** 偶爾、有時候 – **seldom, rarely** 幾乎不～ – **never** 完全不～

* **regularly** 規律地、定期地

early 及早、提早　**late** 晚、遲來地

SENTENCES TO USE

民秀每天傍晚慢跑。	Minsu jogs in the evening every day.
你一整天究竟在做什麼？	What the hell are you doing all day (long)?
我們常開車去鄉下兜風。	We often go driving to the countryside.
近來 K-POP 在全世界很受歡迎。	K-POP is popular all over the world these days.
我現在很忙，沒辦法跟你講話。	I am too busy at the moment to talk with you.
我想起曾經見過那個男生。	I remember seeing him one day.

過去	現在	未來
once upon a time 以前	**recently, lately** 近來	**someday** 未來某天
a long time ago 很久以前	**these days, nowadays** 最近	**in the future** 未來
in the past 過去	**this year** 今年	**next year** 明年
last year 去年	**this month** 這個月	**next month** 下個月
last month 上個月	**this week** 這週	**next week** 下週
last week 上週	**at the moment** 現在	**in an hour** 一小時後
an hour ago 一小時前	**right now** 現在（立刻）	

* **one day** 未來或過去某天
* **sometime**（過去或未來的）某時

late vs. lately
late 可以用作形容詞，表示「晚的」，也可以當副詞，表示「晚」。大家可能會誤會「晚」為 lately，但是 lately 為「近來」，意思完全不同。

sometime vs. sometimes
sometimes 一般用作「有時候、偶爾」的意思，去掉 s 的 sometime 表示「某時」。Let's go skiing sometime.（改天去滑雪。）

once upon a time
once upon a time 為「以前、曾經」的意思，用於描述以前的事情或古老故事的開頭。

three days ago 3天前	the day before yesterday 前天	yesterday 昨天	today 今天	tomorrow 明天	the day after tomorrow 後天

for the first time
一開始

at the beginning of
〜 開始時

in the middle of 〜
〜 途中、〜 時

for the last time
最後

at the end of
〜 結束時

SENTENCES TO USE

你前天見到智敏了吧？	You met Jimin the day before yesterday, didn't you?
我生平第一次搭雲霄飛車。	I've been on a roller coaster for the first time in my life.
我昨天半夜醒來。	I woke up in the middle of the night last night.
他們每週領取薪資。	They are paid weekly.
約莫30年前我住在這一區。	I lived in this neighborhood about three decades ago.

hourly 每個小時（的）   **daily** 每天發生的、每天
weekly 每週的、每週   **monthly** 每月（的）
yearly 每年都有的、每年   **annually** 一年一次
biweekly 隔週的、隔週   **bimonthly** 隔月的、隔月

JANUARY	FEBRUARY	MARCH
M T W T F S S	M T W T F S S	M T W T F S S

APRIL	MAY	JUNE

JULY	AUGUST	SEPTEMBER

OCTOBER	NOVEMBER	DECEMBER

decade 10年   **century** 世紀、100年
millennium 千年
solar calendar 國曆   **lunar calendar** 農曆
leap year 閏年   **leap month** 閏月

使用 every 的表達
every ~ 每～
every other[second] day / week / month 每兩天 / 兩週 / 兩個月
every two days / weeks / months 每兩天 / 兩週 / 兩個月

一次、兩次、三次～
once / twice / three times a day 一天一次 / 兩次 / 三次
once / twice / three times a week 一週一次 / 兩次 / 三次
once / twice / three times a month 一月一次 / 兩次 / 三次

yearly vs. annually
yearly 可以用作形容詞和副詞，annually 只能用作副詞。

This is a yearly event.（形容詞）這是年度活動。
They hold the event yearly.（副詞）他們每年舉辦該活動。
The event is held annually.（副詞）那個活動每年舉辦。

位置

 beside 在～旁邊
next to 緊鄰～
by 在～旁邊

 behind
在～後面

 in front of
在～前面

 beneath
在～正下方

 under, below
在～下面

 on
在～上面

 over, above
在～上面

 on the right / left
在右側 / 左側

on the right / left of
在～的右側 / 左側

 on the opposite side of
在～對面（另一側）

 between A and B
在 A 和 B 之間

 in the middle of
在～中間

 among
在～之間

 inside
在～裡面

 outside
在～外面

 on the corner
在角落

SENTENCES TO USE

他們的別墅在河邊。	Their villa sits by the river.
人們聚集在那家店前面。	People are gathered in front of the store.
孩子們正前往市中心。	The kids were going toward downtown.
書店在街對面。	The bookstore is across[on the opposite side of] the street.
沿路種植著櫻花樹。	Cherry trees are planted along the street.
直走50公尺後請右轉。	Go straight about 50 meters and then turn right.

toward (**s**)
朝～、往～

 across
穿越～、越過～

 into
往～裡面

 out of
往～外面

 through
通過～

 along
沿著～

 turn right
右轉

 turn left
左轉

 go straight
直走、直行

 go upstairs
上樓

go downstairs
下樓

under, below, beneath
- under：特定物體或樓層下方；低於～歲
- below：垂直的兩物體下方；溫度、數量、量～以下（未滿）
- beneath：緊貼於下方

Children under 17 can't see the movie. 17 歲以下的孩子無法觀看那部電影。
Write your answer below the line. 請在線下方填寫答案。
The ship sank beneath the water. 那艘船沉沒至水底。

on, over, above
- on：在某物的表面之上
- over：在～上（移動時、年紀、錢、時間）
- above：在～上（最低值或固定數值）

There was a picture on the wall. 牆上掛了一幅畫。
The dragonfly is flying over the plant. 蜻蜓在植物上飛著。
Mount Everest is 8,848m above sea level. 聖母峰海拔8,848公尺。

數量表達與讀法

數多的	量多的
many 許多的	**much** 許多的
a (large) number of ~大量的	**a large[great, huge] amount of** ~大量的
a lot of ~許多的	**a lot of** ~許多的
lots of ~許多的	**lots of** ~許多的

數少的、少許的	量少的、少許的
some 少的	**some** 少許的
a few 少的	**a little** 少許的
few 幾乎沒有的	**little** 幾乎沒有的
a small number of ~少數的	**a small amount of** ~少量的

SENTENCES TO USE

許多人每年來這座島。	A large number of people visit this island every year.
網路上有大量的資訊。	There is a huge amount of information on the Internet.
請給我幾分鐘時間。	Give me just a few minutes.
我還要再睡一下。	Let me have some more sleep.
我們只剩下一點點錢。	We just have a little money left.
我今天下午吃了一點蛋糕。	I ate a small amount of cake this afternoon.

讀大數字

1,107	one thousand, one hundred and seven
12,345	twelve thousand, three hundred and forty-five
762,815	seven hundred and sixty-two thousand, eight hundred and fifteen
2,053,724	two million, fifty-three thousand, seven hundred and twenty-four
15,000,000	fifteen million
550,000,000	five hundred and fifty million

序數

32nd	thirty second
84th	eighty fourth
103rd	one hundred and third
201st	two hundred and first

讀分數、小數

1/2	a half
1/3	a third, one third
1/4	a quarter, a fourth, one fourth
1/5	a fifth, one fifth
3/4	three quarters, three fourths
1/8	an eighth, one eighth
0.2	(zero) point two
1.5	one point five
4.37	four point three seven

讀日期

4月1日	April first, the first of April
10月23日	October twenty third

讀電話號碼

02-987-6543	zero[o] -two, nine-eight-seven, six-five-four-three
010-8765-4321	zero[o] -one-zero[o] , eight-seven-six-five, four-three-two-one

讀飯店房間號碼

902號	nine o two
315號	three one five

warm, mild
溫暖的、暖和的

sunny 晴朗的
hot 熱的

cloudy 陰的

rainy
下雨的

stormy
下暴風雨的

cool
涼爽的

windy
吹風的

snowy
下雪的

cold 冷的
freezing 寒冷的

SENTENCES TO USE

我希望盡快變溫暖。	I hope it gets warm soon.
韓國的夏天很熱又很潮濕。	Summer in Korea is very hot and humid.
我喜歡陰天。	I like cloudy weather.
我在雨天時多愁善感。	I feel sentimental on rainy days.
今天的氣溫是攝氏零下17度！	Today's temperature is minus 17 degrees Celsius!
起霧時要小心開車。	You should be careful when you drive on a foggy day.

temperature 溫度
(minus) degrees
(Celsius / Fahrenheit)
（零下）（攝氏 / 華氏）～ 度

humidity
濕度

humid
潮濕的

dry
乾燥的

frosty
結霜的

foggy
起霧的

名詞 → 表達天氣的形容詞

sun（太陽）→ sunny
wind（風）→ windy
storm（暴風雨）→ stormy
frost（霜）→ frosty

cloud（雲）→ cloudy
rain（雨）→ rainy
snow（雪）→ snowy
fog（霧）→ foggy

攝氏溫度 (Celsius scale) 和華氏溫度 (Fahrenheit scale)
我們和大部分國家使用的攝氏溫度，以水凝固的0度、沸騰的100度為界，將溫度區分為100等分。攝氏溫度由瑞典的物理學家攝爾修斯設計出，英文以 ~ degrees Celsius 表示。
另一方面，美國和部分歐洲國家使用華氏溫度，以水凝固的32度、沸騰的212度為界，將溫度區分為180等分。華氏溫度由德國的物理學家華倫海特設計出，英文以 ~ degrees Fahrenheit 表示。

（華氏溫度-32）÷1.8=攝氏溫度　　（攝氏溫度×1.8）+32=華氏溫度

raindrop
雨滴

snowflake
雪花

shower
陣雨

storm
暴風雨

thunderstorm
雷雨

lightning 閃電
thunder 打雷

snowstorm
暴風雪

typhoon
颱風

hurricane
龍捲風

SENTENCES TO USE

夏天來場陣雨十分涼爽。	It's refreshing when it showers on a summer day.
一個大颱風正逼近。	A big typhoon is approaching.
這個地區連續多月飽受乾旱之苦。	This area has been suffering from drought for months.
今天也發布了酷暑警報。	A heat wave warning was issued again today.
因為昨晚是熱帶夜，所以我沒睡好覺。	I couldn't sleep well last night either because it felt like a tropical night.
我們今天因為微塵而無法外出。	We can't go outside today because of the fine dust.

flood
洪水

drought
乾旱

heat wave 酷暑
tropical night 熱帶夜

cold wave
寒流

fine dust 微細粉塵
yellow dust 黃沙、沙塵 / **smog** 煙霧

氣象特報、警報

• 天氣特報：watch
颱風特報／警報：a typhoon ~
酷暑特報／警報：a heat wave ~
大雪特報／警報：a heavy-snow (fall) ~

• 警報：warning, alert
豪雨特報／警報：a heavy rain (fall) ~
寒流特報／警報：a cold wave ~
臭氧特報／警報：an ozone ~

發布特報／警報：issue a ~ watch / warning[alert]
解除特報／警報：lift[call off] a ~ watch / warning[alert]
特報／警報生效中：a ~ watch / warning[alert] is in effect

懸浮微粒 PM10, PM2.5

fine dust 是微細粉塵，專業用語為 PM10（懸浮微粒）、PM2.5（細懸浮微粒）。
PM 為 particulate matter 的縮寫，表示懸浮微粒。PM10 表示粒子直徑為10微米以下的懸浮微粒，PM2.5 表示粒子直徑為2.5微米以下的細懸浮微粒。
報導中會使用 PM10、PM2.5，請多加留意。

6 描述事物

大小、長度、重量、高度、距離、深度等

tiny 非常小 → **small** / **little** 小 → **big** / **large** 大 → **huge** 非常大、巨大

short
短的

long
長的、長度〜 長的

high
高的、高度〜 高的

low
矮的

heavy
重的

light
輕的

SENTENCES TO USE

這雙鞋對我來説有點小。	These shoes are a little small for me.
這是全世界最大的電動車公司。	It's the world's biggest electric car company.
那裡以前有棵超級大樹。	There used to be a huge tree there.
首爾最高的山是北漢山。	The highest mountain in Seoul is Bukhansan.
包包不重嗎？要不要幫忙？	Isn't your bag heavy? Do you want me to carry it?
那箱子很輕，我也抬得動。	The box is light enough for me to carry.

thick 厚的			**thin** 薄的
near 近的			**far** 遠的
deep 深的、深度～深的			**shallow** 淺的
wide （幅度或面積）寬的			**narrow** 窄的

SENTENCES TO USE

你的腳踝真細！

Your ankle is really thin!

這裡最近的郵局在哪裡？

Where is the nearest post office from here?

你家到辦公室多遠？

Haw far is it from your house to your office?

這條溪很淺，進去玩也很安全。

This stream is shallow, so it's safe to go in and play.

巴黎的香榭大道是又長又寬廣的街道。

The Champs-Élysées in Paris is a long and wide avenue.

開車穿越窄小的路十分困難。

It's so hard to drive through a narrow path.

狀態

new 新的			**old** 久遠的、舊的
bright 明亮的			**dark** 暗的
hot 熱的			**cold** 冷的
clean 乾淨的 / **tidy, neat** 整齊的、端正的、整潔的			**dirty** 髒的

SENTENCES TO USE

你讀過他的新小説了嗎？	Have you read her new novel?
這條街上有很多老舊的住宅。	There are lots of old houses on this street.
在昏暗的地方讀書對眼睛不好。	They say reading in the dark is not good for the eyes.
這碗湯太燙了，喝不了。	This soup is too hot to eat.
珍的房間總是很乾淨整潔。	Jin's room is always clean and tidy.
請清洗你那雙骯髒的運動鞋。	Please wash your dirty sneakers.

loud
吵雜的

quiet 安靜的、平穩的、少話的
silent 寧靜的、沉默的、寂靜的
still 安靜的、靜止的

hard
堅硬的、堅固的

soft
柔軟的

rough
粗糙的、表面不平整的

smooth
滑順的、表面平滑的

strong
強壯的、有力的

weak
虛弱的、
無力的

tough
堅強的、堅固的

SENTENCES TO USE

我喜歡在安靜的地方工作。	I like working in a quiet place.
他一出現大家就變安靜。	As he showed up, everyone became silent.
靜水流深（俗諺）。	Still waters run deep.
塗這款乳液會讓皮膚十分滑潤。	This lotion makes your skin feel very smooth.

quiet, silent, still
- quiet：指安靜但有些微噪音的狀態、心情平穩的狀態、清閒的狀態、不太多話的人。
- silent：指幾乎沒有聲音的狀態、沉默的狀態、未發出聲音。
- still：指沒有動作、靜止的狀態。

顏色

white 白色（的）　　**black** 黑色（的）
red 紅色（的）　　**orange** 橘色（的）

yellow 黃色（的）　　**yellow green** 草綠色（**yellow-green** 草綠色的）

green 綠色（的）　　**dark green** 深綠色（**dark-green** 深綠色的）

blue 藍色（的）　　**sky blue** 天空色（**sky-blue** 天空色的）
navy blue 海軍藍色（**navy-blue** 海軍藍色的）

violet 紫羅蘭色（的）　　**purple** 紫色（的）
pink 粉紅色（的）　　**gray** 灰色（的）
brown 褐色（的）
beige 裸色（的）　　**cream** 奶油色（的）
silver 銀色（的）　　**gold** 金色（的）

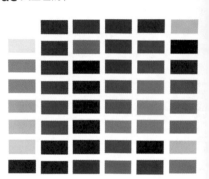

SENTENCES TO USE

由於下大雪，導致全世界都是白色。	It's white everywhere since it snowed a lot.
春天的草綠色葉子真美。	Yellow-green leaves in spring are so pretty.
我穿海軍藍色的套裝去面試。	I went for a job interview wearing a navy-blue suit.
有一首歌叫做〈紫色雨〉，紫色雨究竟是什麼？	There is a song called *Purple Rain*. What is purple rain?
她只穿灰色和黑色衣服。	She only wears gray and black clothes.
這件奶油色襯衫和你很搭。	This cream blouse looks good on you.

wood 木頭、木材
wooden 木頭製的

metal
金屬

glass
玻璃

plastic
塑膠、塑膠製的

paper
紙張

fabric
布料

leather
皮革

rubber
橡膠、橡膠製的

SENTENCES TO USE

木製筷子很輕所以很好用。	Wooden chopsticks are light so they are good to use.
我想要金屬製的手錶。	I'd like to have a metal watch.
羅浮宮前面有巨大的玻璃金字塔。	There's a big glass pyramid in front of the Louvre Museum.
我們應該盡量不要使用塑膠袋。	We shouldn't use plastic bags if it's possible.
大家在演唱會上丟紙飛機。	People flew paper planes at the concert.
皮革包太重了，我提不動。	I can't carry a leather bag since it's heavy.

評斷事物

amazing, awesome, excellent, fantastic, wonderful 了不起的、帥氣的、優秀的
annoying, irritating 煩人的
boring 無趣的
comfortable 舒服的、舒適的、安逸的 (↔ **uncomfortable**)
convenient 方便的、簡便的 (↔ **inconvenient**)
dangerous 危險的
disappointing 使失望的
disgusting 使討厭的、使厭惡的
exciting 使興奮的、使興致滿滿的
frightening, scary 可怕的
fun 有趣的、愉快的

SENTENCES TO USE

那部電影很無聊。	That movie was so boring.
這張椅子非常舒適。	This chair is so comfortable.
這台掃地機器人非常方便。	This robot vacuum cleaner is very convenient.
選舉結果令人十分失望。	The results of the election are quite disappointing.
那個男子說話很令人討厭。	The man's language is too disgusting.
我不看恐怖電影。	I can't watch scary movies.

funny 搞笑的、有趣的　　　　　　　**harmful** 有害的 (↔ **harmless**)
important 重要的　　　　　　　　　**interesting** 有趣的、引人興趣的
pleasant 心情好的、開心的、愉快的 (↔ **unpleasant**)
satisfying 使滿足的　　　　　　　　**shocking** 使震驚的、無法言語的
strange 奇怪的、陌生的　　　　　　**surprising** 使驚訝的
terrible 可怕的、糟糕的　　　　　　**terrific** 很好的、優秀的、帥氣的
useful 有用的 (↔ **useless**)

SENTENCES TO USE

那齣情境喜劇真的很好笑。　　　　That sitcom is really funny.

保健食品若吃太多可能有害健康。　Taking too many food supplements can be harmful to our health.

那間餐廳的餐點讓人很滿意。　　　The meal at the restaurant was very satisfying.

今天聽到一個令人震驚的故事。　　Today I heard a very shocking story.

那位演員的演技很糟糕。　　　　　The actor's performance was terrible.

你為什麼買這種沒用的東西？　　　Why did you buy this useless thing?

心情

delighted, glad, happy, pleased
開心的、愉快的

angry, furious
生氣的

annoyed, irritated
惱人的

anxious, worried
擔心的、不安的

blue, depressed 憂鬱的
disappointed 失望的
embarrassed
困窘的、不好意思的

nervous 緊張的、焦慮的
stressed 有壓力的
upset 傷心的、沮喪的

satisfied
滿足的

surprised
驚訝的

SENTENCES TO USE

別太擔心。	Don't be worried about it too much.
我心情憂鬱了好幾天。	I've been feeling blue for days.
我對他的反應很失望。	I was disappointed with his reaction.
因為沒有帶錢所以我很困窘。	I was embarrassed because I had no money with me.
我緊張的時候會咬指甲。	I bite my fingernails when I'm nervous.
我最近壓力非常大。	I'm so stressed these days.

身體狀態

well 健康的、身體狀況好的
healthy 健康的
strong 強壯的、健壯的

unhealthy 不健康的
weak 虛弱的
ill, sick 生病的

tired 疲勞的
exhausted 身體疲勞的、精疲力竭的
burnt-out 極度疲勞的、疲倦不堪的

SENTENCES TO USE

我今天身體狀況不太好。	I don't feel well today.
幸好我們家的孩子都很健康。	Thankfully all my kids are healthy.
她從小就身體虛弱。	She has been weak since she was a child.
不舒服的時候要吃藥休息。	When you are sick, take medicine and get some rest.
今天過度工作，現在精疲力盡。	I overworked today and now I'm exhausted.
他疲倦不堪，需要休息。	He is burnt-out. He needs some rest.

9 日常生活

wake up
醒來

get up
起床

wash one's face
洗臉

shave
刮鬍子

take a shower
淋浴

wash one's hair
洗頭

dry one's hair
吹頭髮

brush〔comb〕one's hair
梳頭髮

brush one's teeth
刷牙

floss one's teeth
用牙線潔牙

SENTENCES TO USE

她每天洗兩次澡。	She takes a shower twice every day.
睡前最好能吹乾頭髮。	You'd better dry your hair before going to bed.
我刷牙後通常會用牙線清理牙縫。	I always floss my teeth after brushing them.
我化妝只花5分鐘。	It only takes me five minutes to put on my makeup.
我們吃完早餐後上班。	We go to work after having breakfast.
我每天早上8點搭地鐵。	I take the subway at eight every morning.

put on (one's) makeup
化妝

get dressed
穿衣服

eat [have] breakfast
吃早餐

have coffee / tea
喝咖啡 / 茶

take the bus / subway
搭公車 / 地鐵

drive to work
開車上班

go to work
上班

wake up vs. get up
- wake up：醒來
- get up：從床上起來、坐著或躺著後起來

清潔牙齒
- brush one's teeth：刷牙
- floss one's teeth, use dental floss：用牙線潔牙
- use an interdental brushes：使用牙間刷

eat [have] lunch
吃午餐

have [take] a break
休息片刻

finish work
結束工作

**leave [get off] work,
leave the office,
leave for the day**
下班

work overtime
加班

cook [make] dinner
做晚餐

eat [have] dinner
吃晚餐

SENTENCES TO USE

我在員工餐廳吃午餐。	I have lunch at my company cafeteria.
你通常幾點下班？	What time do you usually leave work?
我最近不常加班。	I don't work overtime often these days.
我一週去健身房運動三到四次。	I work out at the gym three or four times a week.
我吃完晚餐後會瀏覽社群媒體或看電視。	After eating dinner, I check social media or watch TV.
我姊姊每天晚上泡澡。	My sister takes a bath every night.

watch TV
看電視

listen to music
聽音樂

work out (at the gym)
（在健身房）運動

**browse[surf]
the Internet**
上網

**check
social media[SNS]**
瀏覽社群媒體

**read a
book / magazine**
看書 / 雜誌

take a bath
泡澡

take a half[lower]-body bath
洗半身浴

go to bed
睡覺

eat, have + 餐點
表示「吃早餐、午餐、晚餐」時，可以使用動詞 eat 和 have。不過要表示吃特定食物時通常會用 eat。

下班
要表示「下班」，可以用 leave work、get off work、leave the office、leave for the day 等，也可以用 finish work，不過這個字比起「下班」之意，更接近單純「結束工作」的意思。換句話說，如果不在辦公室，但完成了某工作，這時候就不用 leave work，選用 finish work 更為適當。

瀏覽社群媒體
社群媒體又可以簡稱為 SNS，美國、加拿大等英語系國家則普遍使用 social media。「瀏覽社群媒體」為 check social media（check SNS 這個表達並非錯誤），在口語中也可以用作 check (out) one's Facebook / Twitter / Instagram（瀏覽臉書 / 推特 / Instagram）。

10 家務事

cook[make] breakfast / lunch / dinner
做早餐 / 午餐 / 晚餐

make a lunchbox
準備便當

set the table
備好餐桌

clear the table
清理餐桌

wash[do] the dishes
洗碗

separate trash
分類垃圾

take out the trash
丟垃圾

clean the house / room / bathroom
打掃家裡 / 房間 / 浴室

clean up one's room / desk
整理房間 / 書桌

vacuum the floor
吸地板

sweep the floor
掃地

mop the floor
拖地

SENTENCES TO USE

我吃完飯後立刻洗碗。	I wash the dishes right after I eat.
丟垃圾是我們家老大的工作。	Taking out the trash is my eldest child's job.
我每天用吸塵器吸地板。	I vacuum the floor every other day.
家事中我最討厭燙衣服。	I hate ironing the most among housework.
我幾乎每天帶我們家小狗去散步。	I walk my dog almost every day.
我一週大約採購食品雜貨兩次。	I do grocery shopping about twice a week.

**do the laundry,
wash the clothes**
洗衣服

**hang
the clothes**
晾衣服

**fold
the clothes**
摺衣服

do the ironing
燙衣服
iron～燙～

make the bed
整理床鋪

**change
the sheets**
換床單

**water
the plants**
澆花

**feed the pet
/ dog / cat**
餵寵物 / 狗 / 貓

walk the dog
遛狗

do the shopping
購物

**do grocery
shopping**
採購（食材）

家務事
「家務事、家事」為 housework、household chores，「做家事」為 do housework、
do household chores。

grocery, groceries
grocery (store, shop) 指販售食品和雜貨的店家，幾乎等同超級市場 (supermarket)。
groceries 指的是食品和雜貨。

11 紀念日、活動

國家重要紀念日

New Year's Day 元旦
Lunar New Year's Day 過年、春節
Arbor Day 植木節
Children's Day 兒童節
Parents'Day 父母節
Buddha's Birthday 佛誕節
Memorial Day（美）陣亡將士紀念日
Constitution Day 行憲記念日
Liberation Day 解放日
Christmas (Day) 聖誕節
New Year's Eve 12月31日

SENTENCES TO USE

韓國最大的兩個節日是春節和中秋。	The two biggest holidays in Korea are Lunar New Year's Day and Chuseok.
行憲紀念日並非假日，你要去上學。	Constitution Day is not a holiday. You have to go to school.
今年的韓文節在週日。	This year, Hangul Proclamation Day falls on Sunday.
我今天要去朋友家的喬遷宴。	I'm going to a friend's housewarming party today.
我這週有三場尾牙。	I have three year-end parties this week alone.
明天是爸爸逝世二週年。	Tomorrow is the second anniversary of my father's death.

個人的紀念日、活動

100th day after birth 嬰兒出生百日
the first birthday 周歲
the sixtieth birthday 六十大壽
the seventieth birthday 七十大壽
wedding anniversary 結婚紀念日
housewarming party 喬遷宴
farewell party 送別會
welcome party 歡迎會
year-end party 尾牙、年終派對
anniversary of one's death 忌日

國定假日

「國定假日」為 national holiday，法定假日為 legal holiday、official (national) holiday。補假（國定假日遇到假日則補假）為 substitute holiday。

CHAPTER

2

人

——

Human

人的身體 (1) - 外部：全身

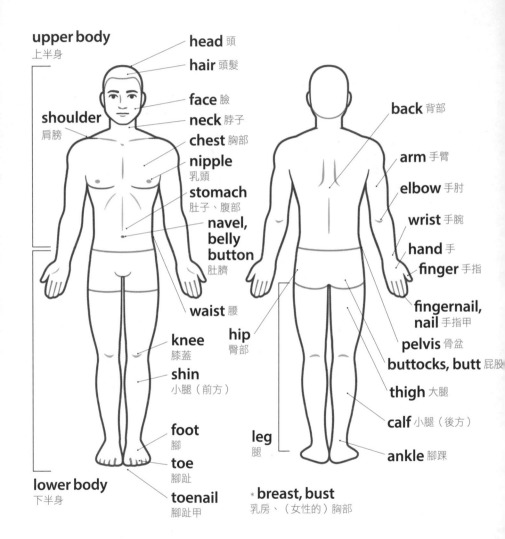

upper body
上半身

head 頭

hair 頭髮

face 臉

neck 脖子

chest 胸部

nipple
乳頭

stomach
肚子、腹部

navel,
belly
button
肚臍

shoulder
肩膀

waist 腰

knee
膝蓋

hip
臀部

shin
小腿（前方）

foot
腳

leg
腿

toe
腳趾

lower body
下半身

toenail
腳趾甲

back 背部

arm 手臂

elbow 手肘

wrist 手腕

hand 手

finger 手指

fingernail,
nail 手指甲

pelvis 骨盆

buttocks, butt 屁股

thigh 大腿

calf 小腿（後方）

ankle 腳踝

* **breast, bust**
乳房、（女性的）胸部

SENTENCES TO USE

我媽媽的下半身比上半身無力。	My mom's lower body is weaker than her upper body.
我下半身肥胖。	I am overweight in my lower body.
年紀越大，下半身的運動越重要。	Exercising your lower body gets important as you get older.
那個男子的肩膀寬闊。	The man has broad shoulders.
請趴下。	Lie on your stomach, please.
那個男子的手指又細又長。	The man has long, thin fingers.

chest vs. breast, bust
chest 指胸部，不分男女。另外，breast 和 bust 指女性的胸部，也就是乳房。

waist vs. back
waist 和 back 都可翻譯為「腰」，容易造成混淆。waist 指的是胸部和臀部間的部位，back 則指後腰。

hips vs. buttocks
hips 和 buttocks 都可翻譯為「臀部」，不過 hips 指的是腰和腿間的骨盆部位（從前面看得到的地方），buttocks 指的是坐著的時候貼著地面的部位（從後面和側面看得到的地方）。換句話說，我們所稱的「屁股」，其實是 buttocks。

人的身體 (2) - 外部：臉、手、腳

臉 **face** 臉

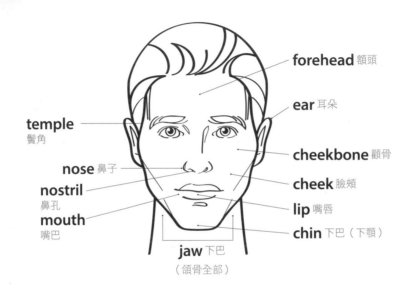

forehead 額頭

ear 耳朵

temple
鬢角

cheekbone 顴骨

nose 鼻子

cheek 臉頰

nostril
鼻孔

lip 嘴唇

mouth
嘴巴

chin 下巴（下顎）

jaw 下巴
（頜骨全部）

眼睛 **eye** 眼睛

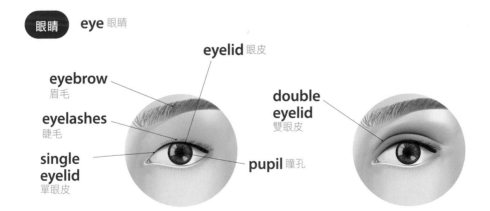

eyelid 眼皮

eyebrow
眉毛

**double
eyelid**
雙眼皮

eyelashes
睫毛

**single
eyelid**
單眼皮

pupil 瞳孔

牙齒 **tooth**（複數 **teeth**）牙齒

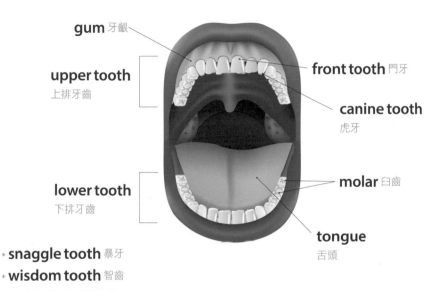

gum 牙齦

upper tooth
上排牙齒

front tooth 門牙

canine tooth
虎牙

lower tooth
下排牙齒

molar 臼齒

tongue
舌頭

* **snaggle tooth** 暴牙
* **wisdom tooth** 智齒

SENTENCES TO USE

他的額頭很寬。	He has a wide forehead.
我的嘴唇總是很乾。	My lips are always dry.
那個嬰兒的睫毛非常長。	The baby has very long eyelashes.
我喜歡單眼皮。	I like single eyelid eyes.
我的臼齒有點蛀牙。	I have some cavities in my molars.
你有拔過智齒嗎？	Have you ever had a wisdom tooth taken out?

手　**hand** 手

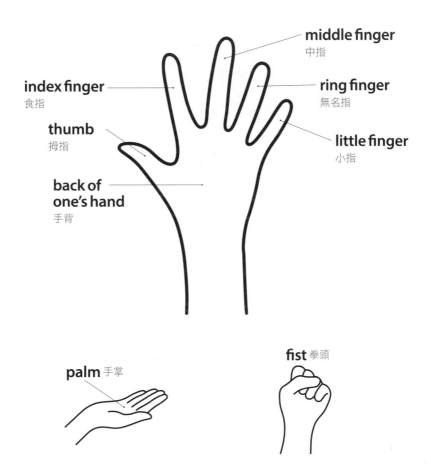

middle finger
中指

index finger
食指

ring finger
無名指

thumb
拇指

little finger
小指

**back of
one's hand**
手背

palm 手掌

fist 拳頭

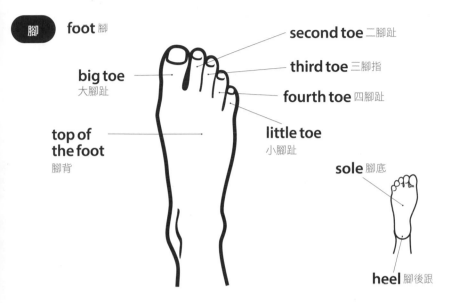

腳　foot 腳

second toe 二腳趾

third toe 三腳指

big toe
大腳趾

fourth toe 四腳趾

top of
the foot
腳背

little toe
小腳趾

sole 腳底

heel 腳後跟

SENTENCES TO USE

那位男子用手背擦額頭的汗。 | The man wiped the sweat off his forehead with the back of his hand.

我把他的電話號碼寫在手掌上。 | I wrote down his phone number on my palm.

戒指通常戴第四根手指頭。 | We usually wear a ring on our ring finger.

蚊子叮了我的腳底！ | A mosquito bit my sole!

我應該要去除腳後跟的角質。 | I should get rid of the dead skin on my heel.

你的第二根腳趾頭比大腳趾還長！ | Your second toe is longer than your big toe!

3 人的身體 (3) - 內部

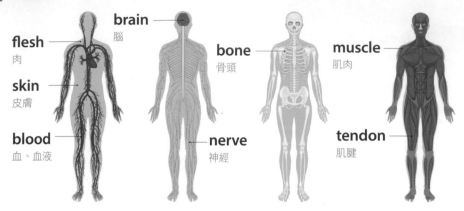

brain
腦

flesh
肉

skin
皮膚

blood
血、血液

bone
骨頭

nerve
神經

muscle
肌肉

tendon
肌腱

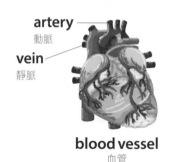

artery
動脈

vein
靜脈

blood vessel
血管

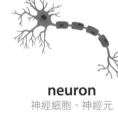

neuron
神經細胞、神經元

cell
細胞

SENTENCES TO USE

我應該做肌力運動。	I have to work out my muscles.
我喉嚨痛,沒辦法好好說話。	I have a sore throat and I can't speak well.
我的狗自幼心臟虛弱。	My dog has a weak heart from birth.
如果你的肝不好,會很容易疲倦。	If your liver isn't good, you'll get tired easily.
我奶奶膝蓋關節不好, 因此去動手術。	My grandmother got surgery on her knee joint since it was so bad.

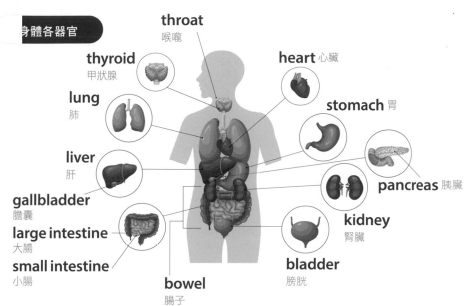

身體各器官

throat 喉嚨

thyroid 甲狀腺

heart 心臟

lung 肺

stomach 胃

liver 肝

pancreas 胰臟

gallblabber 膽囊

kidney 腎臟

large intestine 大腸

small intestine 小腸

bladder 膀胱

bowel 腸子

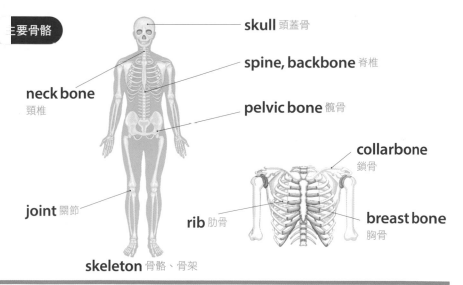

主要骨骼

skull 頭蓋骨

spine, backbone 脊椎

neck bone 頸椎

pelvic bone 髖骨

collarbone 鎖骨

joint 關節

rib 肋骨

breast bone 胸骨

skeleton 骨骼、骨架

身體的各種分泌物

tear 眼淚	sweat 汗	saliva 口水
phlegm 痰	sleep 眼屎	earwax 耳屎
urine, pee 尿	feces, excrement, stool 大便	

體型、風格

short
個子矮的

medium height 個子中等（的）
average height 平均身高（的）

tall
個子高的

slim, slender
苗條的、纖細的

skinny, thin
過瘦的、瘦的

chubby
胖的

overweight
過重的

obese
肥胖的

muscular
肌肉發達的

fat
胖的

SENTENCES TO USE

我中等身高，微胖。	I am medium height and a little chubby.
我有位朋友因為太瘦而煩惱。	A friend of mine is worried since she is too skinny.
體重過重並非絕對不好吧？	Being overweight isn't necessarily a bad thing, is it?
我姊姊生孩子後變得過胖。	My sister became obese after giving birth to a child.
那對老夫妻一起在遊輪上旅行。	The elderly couple is on a cruise together.
我看到她前幾天和帥氣的男子走在一起。	I saw her walking with a good-looking man the other day.

 **middle-aged** 中年的

 **old** 老的、年紀大的
（**elderly** 年長的）

good-looking 長得好看的
handsome（主要用於男性）帥的
gorgeous 漂亮的、有魅力的
attractive 有魅力的
beautiful（主要用於女性或孩子）美麗的
pretty 漂亮的、可愛的
lovely 惹人喜愛的、具魅力的

體重相關表達

- gain weight：增胖
- lose weight：減肥
- be on a diet：減重中

年齡層表達

10多歲：teens	20多歲：twenties	30多歲：thirties
40多歲：forties	50多歲：fifties	60多歲：sixties
70多歲：seventies	80多歲：eighties	90多歲：nineties

- 初期：one's early ~
  I met her in her early thirties. 我在她30幾歲時認識她。
- 中期：one's mid ~
  He wrote the novel in his mid-twenties. 他在25歲左右時寫了那部小説。
- 後期：one's late ~
  They are in their late forties. 他們將近50歲。
- 同年：about[around] one's age
  The actress is about my age. 那位演員和我同年。

5 臉部與髮型

UNIT

臉、皮膚　have + ~ skin / face

pale skin
膚色蒼白、白皙

fair skin
膚色白

tan skin
古銅色皮膚

dark skin
膚色黑

a round face
圓臉

an oval-shaped face
蛋型臉

a thin [an oblong] face
長臉

a square face
四方臉

pimple
青春痘、粉刺

wrinkle
皺紋

dark circles
黑眼圈

acne
青春痘

freckle
雀斑

dry skin
乾性皮膚

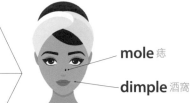

mole 痣

dimple 酒窩

* **oily sin** 油性皮膚

SENTENCES TO USE

那個女生的皮膚很白。	The girl had very fair skin.
真希望我的臉是蛋型臉。	I wish I had an oval-shaped face.
紅髮安妮臉上有雀斑。	Anne of Green Gables has freckles on her face.
我的皺紋越來越多，很煩惱。	I'm distressed I'm getting more and more wrinkles.
我肚臍旁邊有痣。	I have a mole next to my belly button.
他有個迷人的酒窩。	He has a very charming dimple.

60　**CHAPTER 2**　HUMAN

髮型 have + ~ **hair**

long hair
長髮
straight hair
直髮

short hair
短髮

shoulder-length hair
及肩髮

wavy hair
波浪髮

curly hair
捲髮

gray hair
白髮

wear a pony tail
綁馬尾

have one's hair cut
剪頭髮

have one's hair permed
燙頭髮

have one's hair dyed
染頭髮

lose one's hair
掉頭髮

be bald
禿頭

have beard / mustache / sideburns
有鬍子 / 鬍髭 / 鬢角

SENTENCES TO USE

我留了好幾年長髮。	I have had long hair for several years.
那個男生是捲髮。	The boy has curly hair.
你多久剪一次頭髮？	How often do you have your hair cut?
我昨天燙了頭髮。	I had my hair permed yesterday.
我最近掉很多頭髮。	I'm losing a lot of hair these days.
那個男子有鬢角。	The man had sideburns.

動作 (1) - 臉和頭

breathe
呼吸

hold one's breath
憋氣

sigh
嘆氣

yawn
打哈欠

cough
咳嗽

sneeze
打噴嚏

hiccup
打嗝
（**hiccups** 連續打嗝）

wink
眨眼（一側）
blink 眨眼（兩側）

smile
微笑

laugh
大笑

frown
皺眉

cry
哭泣

weep
流淚

SENTENCES TO USE

別嘆氣了。	Stop sighing.
我頭痛就會一直打哈欠。	I keep yawning when I have a headache.
他咳嗽好幾天了。	He's been coughing for days.
我要怎麼做才能停止打嗝？	How can I stop the hiccups?
那個男子對你眨眼嗎？	Did the man wink at you?
你為什麼對我皺眉？	Why are you frowning at me?

look back
回頭看

nod
點頭

shake one's head
搖頭

lower one's head
低頭

one's nose runs
流鼻水

blow one's nose
擤鼻子

wipe one's nose
擦鼻子

pick one's nose
挖鼻孔

spit
吐口水

spit out phlegm
吐痰

whisper
耳語

shout
高喊

SENTENCES TO USE

她回頭看好幾次。 She kept looking back over and over again.

敏浩安靜地點了頭。 Minho nodded quietly.

我的鼻水流不停。 My nose keeps running.

你可不可以停止挖鼻屎？ Why don't you stop picking your nose?

不能在路上吐口水。 You should not spit on the street.

別這麼大聲，我聽得到。 Don't shout. I can hear you.

7 動作 (2) - 身體

raise one's hand
舉手

wave
揮手

clap one's hands
拍手

shake hands with ~
和 ～ 握手

fold one's arms
雙手抱胸

carry
提、拿、攜帶

pick up
提起、撿起

touch
觸摸

SENTENCES TO USE

有問題請舉手。	If you have a question, please raise your hand.
請大家掌聲鼓勵！	Everybody, clap your hands!
那位政治人物今天和超過500個人握手。	The politician shook hands with over 500 people today.
以手指指人是沒禮貌的行為。	Pointing at a person with a finger is rude behavior.
我丟包包，接好！	I'll throw the bag. Catch it!
這扇門要用拉的才能開。	You should pull this door to open.

point (at)
指

hold
握住、抓著

hit
打

lift
抬起

throw
丟

catch
抓住（在動的物體）

pull
拉

push
推

squeeze
擠、捏

twist
扭、轉

兩手交叉

- fold one's arms：自己雙手交叉抱胸
  He talked with his arms folded. 他手抱胸講話。
- link arms with ~ / link arms together：和別人手勾著手
  The girls walked along the street linking arms together.
  女孩們勾著手走在路上。

carry vs. hold

- carry：攜帶、運送（移動之意）
  The man was carrying a briefcase. 那個男子帶著公事包。
- hold：（用手）抓著、握著、拿著（沒有移動之意）
  She was holding a teddy bear. 她抓著熊娃娃。

pick up vs. lift

- pick up：撿起在地上的東西
  He picked up a small pebble. 他撿了一塊小石頭。
- lift：抬起、抬起後放下
  She lifted her face from a book. 她讀了一會書後抬起頭。

lie
躺

lie on one's face[stomach]
趴

stand up
起立

fall down
跌倒

bow
彎腰（低頭）打招呼

shrug
聳肩

shiver
顫抖

hug, embrace
擁抱

walk
走路

SENTENCES TO USE

我那時候趴著讀雜誌。	I lied on my stomach and was reading a magazine then.
小心不要跌倒。	Please be careful not to fall down.
韓國人見面時通常彎腰打招呼。	Koreans usually bow when they meet with each other.
他聳肩不說話。	He shrugged and said nothing.
她常常擁抱他人。	She often hugs people.
我每天走一萬步以上。	I walk more than 10,000 steps every day.

run
跑

jump
跳

kneel (down)
跪

kick
踢

crawl
（趴著）爬

climb
爬

bend one's knees
屈膝

tiptoe, walk on tiptoe
踮腳尖走路

SENTENCES TO USE

別在手扶梯上奔跑。　　　　　Do not run on escalators.

他們跪著祈禱。　　　　　　　They knelt down and prayed.

請把那個球踢給我。　　　　　Please kick that ball to me.

那個嬰兒最近用手和膝蓋爬行。　The baby crawls on hands and knees these days.

我覺得爬階梯很辛苦。　　　　It's hard for me to climb the stairs.

我踮著腳走路，怕媽媽醒過來。　I walked on tiptoe in case my mother woke up.

8 個性和態度

active
活躍的、積極的

arrogant
傲慢的

bold
大膽的、勇敢的

brave
勇敢的

careful
仔細的、小心的

cheerful
快活的、開心的

confident
有自信的

considerate
體貼的、體諒的

curious
具好奇心的

diligent
勤奮的、勤勉的

friendly
親切的、和藹的

funny
搞笑的、有趣的

SENTENCES TO USE

潤秀比她的外表看起來還要活躍。	Yunsu is more active than she looks.
他非常有自信。	He is very confident of himself.
敏非常體貼。	Min is so considerate.
要常常對他人慷慨。	Always try to be generous to others.
有點衝動是他的缺點。	Being a little impulsive is his weakness.
他非常謙遜。	He is very modest.

generous	gentle	honest	impulsive
慷慨的、寬厚的	溫和的、親切的、和善的	正直的、老實的	衝動的

industrious	intelligent	jealous	kind
勤勉的、勤勞的	聰明的、知性的	忌妒的、猜忌的	親切的

lazy	mature	mean	modest
懶惰的	成熟的	卑鄙的、小氣的	謙遜的、端莊的

加字首變成反義字

active	↔	inactive	不活躍的、消極的
confident	↔	unconfident	沒有信心的
considerate	↔	inconsiderate	不體貼的
friendly	↔	unfriendly	不友好的、不親切的
generous	↔	ungenerous	吝嗇的、不大方的
honest	↔	dishonest	不正直的
kind	↔	unkind	不親切的、不近人情的
mature	↔	immature	不成熟的、幼稚的

negative 負面的、悲觀的
obstinate, stubborn 固執的
open-minded 開放的、沒有偏見的
optimistic 樂觀的、樂天的
outgoing 外向的、社交的
passionate 熱情的
passive 被動的、消極的
patient 有耐心的、有毅力的
pessimistic 悲觀的、厭世的
polite 有禮貌的、謙遜的
positive 正向的
proud 自豪的、有自尊心的

SENTENCES TO USE

我沒看過那麼固執的人。	I've never seen anyone so stubborn.
那個男孩非常外向。	The boy is very outgoing.
你超有耐心！	You are so patient!
她是很理性的人。	She is quite a reasonable person.
智浩總是很認真。	Jiho is always serious.
我太小心翼翼，沒辦法做那種事。	I am too timid to do such a thing.

reasonable 理性的、通情達理的
reliable 值得信賴的
responsible 有責任感的
rude 無理的、沒禮貌的
selfish 自私的
sensitive 細心的、敏感的
serious 嚴肅的、認真的
shy 害羞的
silly, foolish, stupid 傻的、笨的
thoughtful 思考周全的、體貼的
timid 小心的、沒有勇氣的、懼怕的
wise 有智慧的、賢明的、機智的

加字首變成反義字

patient	↔	impatient	沒有耐心的
polite	↔	impolite	無禮的、粗魯的
reasonable	↔	unreasonable	不合理的、不當的
reliable	↔	unreliable	無法信賴的
responsible	↔	irresponsible	沒責任感的
selfish	↔	unselfish	不自私的、無私心的
thoughtful	↔	unthoughtful	思考不周全的、不注意的
wise	↔	unwise	不明智的、傻的

9 情緒

正面的情緒

delighted 開心的
excited 興奮的
grateful, thankful 感謝的
happy 開心的、愉快的
interested 感興趣的
pleased 喜悅的、滿足的
proud 自豪的
relaxed 放鬆的、悠閒的
satisfied 滿足的
thrilled 很開心的、非常興奮的

SENTENCES TO USE

很開心再次見到你。	I'm so delighted to meet you again.
他去到遊樂園非常興奮。	He is so excited to go to the amusement park.
謝謝你待我這麼親切。	I'm grateful that you treated me kind.
我真自豪有你這樣的朋友。	I'm proud to have a friend like you.
走在森林裡讓我心情放鬆。	Walking through the forest makes me feel relaxed.
你滿意自己的生活嗎？	Are you satisfied with your life?

負面的情緒

angry 生氣的
annoyed, irritated 惱人的、煩躁的
anxious 不安的、憂慮的
bored 無聊的
confused 不清楚的、混亂的
concerned 擔心的、憂慮的
depressed 憂鬱的
disappointed 失望的
embarrassed 困窘的
exhausted 精疲力盡的
frightened 害怕的、恐懼的
frustrated 有挫折感的、不滿的

furious 極度生氣的
lonely 孤獨的
miserable 悲慘的、慘淡的
nervous 不安的、焦慮的、緊張的
shocked 受衝擊的、震驚的
stressed 有壓力的
tired 疲勞的
unhappy 不開心的、不滿的
upset 傷心的、沮喪的
worried 擔心的、憂愁的

*__surprised__ 驚訝的（中立用語）

SENTENCES TO USE

她一直干涉，我覺得很煩。	I am annoyed that she keeps interfering.
我不清楚他說的話是什麼意思。	I'm confused about what he said.
我因為你感到很困窘。	I was embarrassed because of you.
大家都因為那位年輕歌手突如其來的死亡感到震驚。	Everyone was shocked at the young singer's sudden death.
他很容易有壓力。	He gets easily stressed.
別因為那件事太傷心。	Don't be too upset about it.

CHAPTER

3

服装

Clothing

各類服裝

 dress shirt
男性正裝襯衫

 T-shirt
T 恤

 blouse
女性襯衫

 sweatshirt
運動衫

 hoody
連帽上衣

 sweater
毛衣

 cardigan
羊毛衫

 vest
背心

 jacket
夾克

 coat
外套、大衣

 padding
羽絨衣

 suit
套裝

 dress
洋裝

 skirt
裙子

 pants
褲子

SENTENCES TO USE

佑民喜歡連帽上衣。	Yumin likes hoodies.
這種天氣你最好要準備羊毛衫。	You'd better pack a cardigan in this weather.
牛仔褲適合搭任何上衣。	Jeans go well with any top.
我今天買了新運動服。	I bought a new training suit today.
他不太打領帶。	He rarely wears a tie.
我手洗內衣。	I wash my underwear by hand.

jeans
牛仔褲

 shorts
短褲

 **training suit, sportswear**
運動服

 pajamas
睡衣

 bathrobe
浴袍

 tie
領帶

 socks
襪子

 leggings
內搭褲

 panty hose
褲襪

 stockings
長筒襪、絲襪

 underwear
內衣

 bra
內衣、胸罩

 panties
（女性、兒童用）
內褲

 underpants
（男性用）內褲

 **boxer shorts**
（男性用）四角褲

* **undershirt** 汗衫、貼身內衣

衣服的細部裝飾

collar 衣領　　　　　sleeve 袖子　　　　　button 釦子
cuffs button 袖扣　　　hood（在外套等後方的）帽子
zipper 拉鍊　　　　　pocket 口袋

衣服相關動詞表達
- wear：穿著、戴著（狀態）
- put on：穿、戴（動作）
- take off：脫
- change：換
- fasten：拉上拉鍊、扣上釦子、戴好別針等（↔ unfasten 解開）

衣服材質、圖案和風格

材質

cotton
棉

silk
絲、絲綢

woolen
羊毛製的

fur
毛皮

polyester
聚酯纖維

leather
皮革

denim
牛仔布、丹寧

linen
亞麻布

nylon
尼龍

紋路

plain
沒有紋路的

striped
條紋的

checkered
格紋的

polka-dot
圓點

各種紋路

- 紋路、圖案：pattern
- 條紋：stripes
- 格紋：checks, checkers, a checkered pattern
- 圓點：polka dots
- 花紋：floral[flower] pattern
- 菱形格紋：argyle pattern（鑽石紋）

030

風格

formal 正式的
neat, tidy 端正的、整齊的

untidy
不修邊幅的

loose
寬鬆的

informal, casual
日常的、休閒的

**fashionable,
stylish, trendy**
流行的、帥氣的、時尚的

tight
緊身的

SENTENCES TO USE

我只能穿棉製的衣服。	I can only wear cotton clothes.
看看那位穿條紋襯衫的男子。	Look at that guy wearing a striped shirt over there.
圓點洋裝很適合你。	A polka-dot dress looks good on you.
你那天可以穿休閒服裝。	You can wear casual clothes that day.
這件 T 恤太過緊。	This T-shirt is too tight.
那個男生很時尚。	The man is very fashionable.

hat
帽子

cap
棒球帽

gloves
手套

handkerchief
手帕

glasses, spectacles
眼鏡

sunglasses
太陽眼鏡

belt
腰帶

watch
手錶

scarf
披巾、圍巾

shawl
披肩

SENTENCES TO USE

陽光很強烈，你要戴帽子。	The sun is so strong that you have to wear a hat.
我的手很冷，所以要戴手套。	My hands are so cold that I have to wear gloves.
我沒繫腰帶，褲子一直往下滑。	My pants keep falling down because I didn't wear my belt.
現在有智慧型手機， 幾乎沒什麼人戴手錶了。	These days not many people wear watches since they have smart phones.
這種天氣我會圍圍巾。	I'll wear a scarf in this weather.
我通常帶著帆布托特包。	I usually carry a canvas tote bag.
雨季我總會隨身攜帶雨傘。	I always carry an umbrella with me during the rainy season.

suitcase
行李箱

briefcase
公事包

backpack
後背包

shoulder bag
肩背包

handbag
手提包

tote bag
托特包

canvas tote bag
帆布托特包

purse, wallet
錢包

umbrella
雨傘

parasol
陽傘

wear ~
- a hat, a cap：戴帽子
- a scarf / a muffler / a shawl：戴圍巾 / 厚圍巾 / 披肩
- gloves：戴手套
- a belt：繫腰帶
- glasses / sunglasses：戴眼鏡 / 太陽眼鏡
- a watch：戴手錶
- a hair pin / a hair tie / a hair band / a necklace / a bracelet / earrings / a ring / a brooch：戴髮夾 / 髮圈 / 髮帶 / 項鍊 / 手鍊 / 耳環 / 戒指 / 胸針

撐雨傘、收雨傘
- put up[hold] an umbrella：撐雨傘
- close[fold] an umbrella：收雨傘
- open an umbrella：開雨傘

purse vs. wallet
purse 和 wallet 都是「錢包」的意思，不過 wallet 是一般能放紙鈔、硬幣、卡片、名片等的對摺型錢包。purse 除了指錢包、長夾，還有手提包的意思。

81

jewelry
珠寶、首飾

necklace
項鍊

bracelet
手鐲

earrings
耳環

ring
戒指

brooch
胸針

hair tie
髮圈

hair band
髮帶、髮箍

hair pin
髮夾

SENTENCES TO USE

那位中年女性佩戴很多首飾。	The middle-aged woman wore lots of jewelry.
我買了銀項鍊要給妹妹。	I bought a silver necklace for my sister.
我比較喜歡小耳環。	I prefer to wear small earrings.
你戴了我不曾見過的戒指。	You wear a ring I haven't seen before.
我媽媽給了我這個胸針。	My mother gave me this brooch.
用髮圈綁一下你的頭髮。	Tie your hair with a hair tie.

sneakers
運動鞋

running shoes
運動鞋、跑步鞋

high heels
高跟鞋

flats, flat shoes
平底鞋

wedge heels
船型鞋

loafers
樂福鞋

sandals
涼鞋

boots
靴子、長靴
（**rain boots** 雨靴）

flip-flops
橡膠拖鞋、夾腳拖

slippers
室內拖鞋

SENTENCES TO USE

穿牛仔褲配運動鞋最舒服。　　　Wearing jeans and sneakers is the most comfortable.

我從來沒有穿過高跟鞋。　　　　I have never worn high heels.

我小時候下雨天穿雨靴。　　　　I wore rain boots on rainy days when I was a child.

別穿室內拖鞋出去。　　　　　　Don't go outside in your slippers.

鞋子的各部位
- heel：跟
- insole：鞋內底
- outsole：皮鞋外底
- bottom of a shoe：鞋底
- shoe lace：鞋帶

UNIT 4 清潔、化妝

take[have] a shower
淋浴

take[have] a bath
泡澡

wash one's face
洗臉

wash one's hair
洗頭

dry one's hair
吹頭髮

do[fix] one's hair
修剪頭髮

tie one's hair back
往後綁頭髮

have one's hair cut
剪頭髮

get a perm, have one's hair permed
燙頭髮

dye one's hair, have one's hair dyed
染頭髮

cut[trim] one's fingernails / toenails
剪（修整）手指甲 / 腳趾甲

put on makeup
化妝

SENTENCES TO USE

我流汗了，要洗個澡。	I've been sweating, so I'll take a shower.
我沒有每天洗頭髮。	I don't wash my hair every day.
整理頭髮很花時間嗎？	Does it take you long to do your hair?
我媽媽每個月染髮。	My mother dyes her hair every month.
我該剪手指甲了。	It's time to cut my fingernails.
她畫淡妝。	She puts on light makeup.

化妝品 **apply, put on** ~抹~

toner	**lotion**	**moisturizer**	**foundation**	**blusher**	**eye shadow**
化妝水	乳液	保濕霜	粉底液	腮紅	眼影

lipstick	**mascara**	**eyeliner**	**aftershave**	**perfume**	**nail polish**	**hair dye**
口紅	睫毛膏	眼線筆	鬍後水	香水	指甲油	染髮劑

浴室用品

comb	**hairbrush**	**shampoo**	**conditioner**
扁梳	梳子	洗髮精	護髮素

shower gel	**face wash**	**facial foaming cleanser**	**soap**	**shaving foam**	**razor**
沐浴乳	洗面乳	泡沫洗面乳	肥皂	刮鬍泡沫	刮鬍刀

toothbrush	**toothpaste**	**interdental brush**	**dental floss**	**mouthwash**	**toilet paper**
牙刷	牙膏	牙間刷	牙線	漱口水	衛生紙

CHAPTER

4

食物

Food

食材 (1) - 穀物和蔬菜

穀類

rice 米
brown rice 糙米
wheat 小麥
barley 大麥
bean, soybean 豆子、大豆
black bean 黑豆
kidney bean 腰豆
pea 碗豆
red bean 紅豆
corn 玉米
rye 黑麥
oat 燕麥
flour 麵粉
whole wheat 全麥

SENTENCES TO USE

糙米和全麥有益健康。

Brown rice and whole wheat are good for your health.

我兒子不吃加了黑豆的飯。

My son doesn't eat rice cooked with black beans.

聽說高麗菜有益腸胃。

They say cabbage is good for your stomach.

我們在自己的菜園種了辣椒和萵苣。

We grow peppers and lettuce in our kitchen garden.

我在咖哩中加馬鈴薯、紅蘿蔔、洋蔥和豬肉。

I put potatoes, carrots, onions and pork in my curry.

如果不加蒜頭，濃湯就會沒味道。

If you don't put garlic in it, the stew doesn't taste good.

蔬菜

Chinese cabbage
大白菜

white radish
蘿蔔

cabbage
高麗菜

lettuce
生菜、萵苣

zucchini
櫛瓜、夏南瓜

pumpkin
（圓的）南瓜

cucumber
小黃瓜

egg plant
茄子

carrot
紅蘿蔔

potato
馬鈴薯

sweet potato
地瓜

green onion, scallion
蔥

onion
洋蔥

leek
韭菜

hot pepper
辣椒

bell pepper, sweet pepper
甜椒

garlic
蒜頭

ginger
生薑

mushroom
蘑菇

bean sprout
豆芽菜

spinach
菠菜

perilla leaf
紫蘇葉

lotus root
蓮藕

2 食材 (2) - 海鮮、肉類、雞蛋

海鮮 **seafood** 海鮮

pollack
明太魚

mackerel
青花魚

cod
鱈魚

anchovy
鯷魚

halibut
大比目魚

trout
鱒魚

tuna
鮪魚

salmon
鮭魚

hairtail, cutlassfish
白帶魚

mackerel pike
秋刀魚

sardine
沙丁魚

seaweed
海藻類

SENTENCES TO USE

海鮮中我最喜歡蝦子。
I like shrimp the most among seafood.

聽說青花魚、秋刀魚等青背魚對身體很好。
They say blue-backed fish like mackerel and mackerel pike are good for your health.

海藻類有助於清血管。
Seaweed helps make our blood clear.

他對牡蠣過敏。
He's allergic to oysters.

我喜歡豬肉勝過牛肉。
I like pork better than beef.

蛋黃富含膽固醇。
Egg yolks contain a lot of cholesterol.

squid
魷魚

octopus
章魚

oyster
牡蠣

clam
蛤、蚌

mussel
淡菜

shrimp
蝦子

crab
螃蟹

lobster
龍蝦

肉類、雞蛋

meat
肉

beef
牛肉

pork
豬肉

lamb
羊肉

chicken
雞肉

duck meat
鴨肉

egg
雞蛋

(egg) yolk
蛋黃

egg white
蛋白

海鮮種類
- blue-backed fish：青背魚
- white meat[fleshed] fish：白肉魚
- saltwater fish：鹹水魚
- freshwater fish：淡水魚

雞肉各部位
breast 雞胸肉　　　　leg 腿 (= drumstick)　　　wing 翅

牛肉、豬肉各部位
sirloin 牛後腰脊肉　　tenderloin 牛里脊肉　　　pork belly 五花肉
beef rib 牛排　　　　pork rib 豬排

食材 (3) - 水果、堅果類

 水果　**fruits** 水果

apple
蘋果

pear
梨子

orange
柳丁

strawberry
草莓

grape
葡萄

peach
桃子

watermelon
西瓜

mandarin
橘子

persimmon
柿子

apricot
杏桃

plum
李子、梅子

grapefruit
葡萄柚

SENTENCES TO USE

早上吃蘋果對健康非常有益。　The apple we eat in the morning is very good for our health.

狗不能吃葡萄。　Dogs shouldn't eat grapes.

我最喜歡的水果？桃子。　My favorite fruit? Peach.

你可以自己在家做柿子乾。　You can make dried persimmons at home.

柳丁和葡萄柚長得很像。　Oranges and grapefruit look alike.

banana
香蕉

mango
芒果

pineapple
鳳梨

kiwi fruit
奇異果

pomegranate
石榴

fig
無花果

jujube
棗子

raisin
葡萄乾

堅果類　**nuts** 堅果類

peanut
花生

chestnut
栗子

almond
杏仁

walnut
核桃

pine nut
松子

SENTENCES TO USE

石榴富含雌激素。　　　　　　Pomegranates contain a lot of female hormones.

每天吃堅果有益健康。　　　　　Eating nuts every day is good for your health.

花生是豆子嗎？　　　　　　　　Are peanuts beans?

水果相關表達
- 摘水果：pick ~
- 剝、削水果：peel ~
- 榨果汁：make juice out of ~
- 果肉：flesh
- 果皮：peel
- 果汁：juice

4 食材 (4) - 乳製品、調味料

乳製品 **dairy[milk] product** 乳製品

milk
牛奶
low fat milk
低脂牛奶

yogurt
優格
fat-free yogurt
零脂優格

cheese
起司

butter
奶油

soybean milk
豆漿

SENTENCES TO USE

牛奶是很好的鈣質來源。	Milk is a great source of calcium.
我不太能消化牛奶。	I can't digest milk.
她在家做優格。	She makes yogurt at home.
橄欖油對身體好。	Olive oil is good for our health.
我媽媽在家做味噌和辣椒醬。	My mom makes soybean paste and red pepper paste at home.
請給我食醋和芥末。	(I'd like some) vinegar and mustard, please.

037

醬料、調味料 **seasoning, condiment** 醬料、調味料

salt 鹽
sugar 砂糖
red pepper powder 辣椒粉
pepper 胡椒
soy sauce 醬油
soybean paste 味噌
red pepper paste 辣椒醬
sesame salt 芝麻鹽
cooking oil 食用油
olive oil 橄欖油
sesame oil 芝麻油
perilla oil 紫蘇油
sesame 芝麻
perilla 紫蘇
vinegar 食醋
mustard 芥末
dressing 調味料
marinade（醃肉等的）醬料

各類飲食

餐點

cooked rice 飯
soup 湯
hot pot 火鍋
braised short ribs 燉排骨
curry and rice 咖哩飯
noodle 麵
instant noodle 泡麵
rice-cake soup 年糕湯
fried egg 煎蛋
scrambled egg 炒蛋
side dishes 小菜

stew 濃湯、燉菜
porridge 粥、燕麥粥
grilled pork belly 烤五花肉
pork / fish cutlet 豬排 / 魚排
fried rice 炒飯
risotto 義大利燉飯
cold noodle 冷麵
handmade noodle 手擀麵、手工麵
dumpling soup 湯餃
sunny side up 半熟蛋
boiled egg 水煮蛋

SENTENCES TO USE

韓式料理基本上有飯和小菜。
Korean food is basically made up of rice and side dishes.

我媽媽沒有湯或濃湯吃不了飯。
My mom can't eat without soup or stew.

他只會做炒飯。
The only dish he can cook is fried rice.

我喜歡所有的麵類。
I like all kinds of noodles.

看到水煮蛋就想到火車旅行。
A boiled egg reminds me of a train trip.

點心、甜點

rice cake
年糕

sponge cake
海綿蛋糕

sandwich
三明治

toast
烤吐司

(plain) bread
（原味）吐司麵包

pastry
油酥糕點

doughnut
甜甜圈

cookie
餅乾

飲料、酒類

sparkling water 氣泡水
brewed coffee 現磨咖啡
hot chocolate 熱巧克力
green tea 綠茶
liquor 烈酒
brew / make coffee 煮咖啡
drunk 醉的
have[suffer from] a hangover 宿醉

soft drink, soda 冷飲、碳酸飲料
instant coffee 即溶咖啡
herbal tea 花草茶
black tea 紅茶
draft beer 生啤酒
make tea 泡茶
sober 未酒醉的

SENTENCES TO USE

年糕和麵包你比較喜歡哪個？	Which do you like better, rice cake or bread?
碳酸飲料也有咖啡因嗎？	Is there caffeine in soft drinks?
喝太多即溶咖啡會變胖。	If you drink too much instant coffee, you can gain weight.
聽說紅茶能溫暖身體。	They say black tea keeps you warm.
他自己煮咖啡。	He brews coffee himself.
我昨晚喝太多酒而宿醉。	I have a hangover since I drank so much last night.

6 料理方式

cut
切

chop
切碎

slice
切薄片

dice, cube
切丁

julienne
切絲

peel
削皮

grate
（用磨碎器）磨

mince
以機器絞肉

mash
搗碎

mix 攪拌
stir 攪拌、拌入

whisk
打泡沫

SENTENCES TO USE

洋蔥切薄片後加橄欖油翻炒。	Slice the onions thinly and stir-fry them in olive oil.
我把蘿蔔切成丁。	I diced a white radish.
請將紅蘿蔔切成細絲。	Julienne carrots, please.
我削馬鈴薯皮時割傷手。	I cut my finger while peeling the potatoes.
請用磨泥器磨一些生薑。	Please grate some ginger.
他以茶匙攪拌咖啡。	He stirred his coffee with a tea spoon.

pour
倒

 blanch
汆燙

 boil
水煮

 steam
蒸

 stir-fry
炒

 fry
炸

 grill
燒烤

 barbecue
炭烤

 roast 以烤箱或火烤
bake 烘焙

SENTENCES TO USE

請將波菜稍微汆燙過。	Blanch spinach a little.
我要煮玉米來吃。	I'm going to boil the corn and eat it.
請將備好的蔬菜以中火翻炒。	Stir-fry prepared vegetables over medium heat.
韓國煎餅要加充足的油去煎才美味。	Korean pancakes are delicious when you fry them with enough oil.
火烤魚最美味。	Fish tastes best when you grill it.
這是我第一次在家烤瑪德蓮。	It's my first time baking madeleines at home.

99

廚房工具、容器

saucepan
長柄含蓋深鍋

frying pan
平底鍋

wok
炒菜鍋

pot
圓鍋

colander
濾盆

bowl
碗

plate
盤子

tray
托盤

jar
廣口瓶、罐

cutting board
砧板

kitchen knife
刀子

scissors
剪刀

peeler
削皮器

spatula, fish slice
鍋鏟

ladle
湯杓

rice paddle
飯勺

SENTENCES TO USE

砧板中我最喜歡木頭製砧板。 Among various cutting boards, a wooden one is best.

我要在哪裡磨我的廚房刀子？ Where can I sharpen my kitchen knife?

剪刀在廚房中有很多用途。 Scissors are useful in the kitchen.

我用削皮器削馬鈴薯皮。 I peeled the potatoes with a peeler.

你煎蛋時需要鍋鏟嗎？ Do you need a spatula when you fry eggs?

用那個飯勺挖飯。 Scoop rice with that rice paddle.

whisk
攪拌器

(kitchen) scales
（廚房）秤子

can opener
開罐器

bottle opener
開瓶器

spoon
湯匙

chopstick
筷子

kettle
茶壺

teacup
茶杯

glass
坡璃朴

mug
馬克杯

apron
圍裙

dishwashing liquid
洗潔精

sponge
（洗碗用）海綿

dishcloth, dishtowel, dishrag
抹布

SENTENCES TO USE

廚房的秤子非常有用。	Scales in the kitchen are useful.
可以給我開瓶器嗎？	Could you give me the bottle opener?
他不太會用筷子。	He's not good at using chopsticks.
穿上圍裙工作，不然衣服會髒。	Work with an apron on. Otherwise, your clothes will get dirty.
我媽媽用天然的廚房洗潔精。	My mother uses natural dishwashing liquid.
我常常消毒抹布。	I often disinfect the dishtowel.

8 味道

動詞

dine 吃飯
taste 品嚐
chew 咀嚼
swallow 吞
bite 咬
sip 啜飲
gulp 大口喝

形容詞

delicious, tasty, yummy, savory 美味的、好吃的
sweet 甜的
salty 鹹的
hot 辣的
sour 酸的

SENTENCES TO USE

品嚐看看是否過淡。	Taste it to see if it is bland.
食物要充分咀嚼。	You should chew your food enough.
吞藥時要小心。	Be careful when you swallow medicine.
今天吃了很多鹹食。	I ate a lot of salty food today.
我超能吃辣的食物。	I have no problem with hot and spicy food.
你懷孕時想吃酸的食物嗎？	Do you want to eat sour food when you're pregnant?

sweet-and-sour
酸酸甜甜的

spicy
味道重的、辣的

oily, greasy
油膩的

crunchy, crispy
酥脆的

mild
味道順口的、溫和的

iced
加冰塊的

bitter
苦的

bland
清淡的

fishy
魚腥味的

chewy
有嚼勁的

strong
味道強烈的、飲料濃的

sparkling, carbonated
有氣泡的、有碳酸的

SENTENCES TO USE

我想吃酸酸甜甜的食物。   I'd like to eat sweet-and-sour food.

這食物有苦味對吧？   This food tastes bitter, doesn't it?

我吃油的東西會拉肚子。   I have loose bowels when I eat greasy food.

我不太能吃有魚腥味的食物。   I find it hard to eat fishy food.

這個炸蔬菜很酥脆。   This fried vegetable is so crispy.

請給我一杯冰咖啡。   Give me a cup of iced coffee.

9 外食

make a reservation 預約
order 點餐
pay the check 結帳
go[do] Dutch 各自付費
dine together 一起吃飯、聚餐
treat 請客
treat somebody to lunch / dinner 請午餐 / 晚餐
takeout (food) 外賣（食物）
~ to go ～（食物）外帶

SENTENCES TO USE

我預約了中式餐廳。	I made a reservation at a Chinese restaurant.
現在可以點餐嗎？	May I order now?
我們那天用餐各自付費。	We went Dutch that day.
這週四我們有小組聚餐。	Our team will dine together this Thursday.
今天晚餐我請客。	I'll treat you to dinner tonight.
請給我外帶一個大的起司披薩。	One large cheese pizza to go, please.

café
咖啡店

restaurant
餐廳

bar
酒吧

fast food restaurant
速食店

buffet
自助餐

cafeteria
自助餐廳

food stall 路邊攤
food truck 食物餐車
course meal 有主菜的套餐
appetizer 開胃菜
main course, entrée 主菜
dessert 點心
today's special 今日特餐
chef's special 主廚特製料理

SENTENCES TO USE

我今天在速食店吃午餐。	I had lunch at a fast food restaurant today.
我去自助餐總是吃太多。	I always overeat at the buffet.
活動上有許多小吃攤。	There are many food stalls at the festival.
你有看過食物餐車嗎？	Have you ever seen a food truck?
今天的主菜是什麼？	What's the main course of the day?
我們吃主廚特製料理吧！	Let's have a chef's special.

CHAPTER

5

住家

Housing

build a house
蓋房

go house hunting
去看房

lease[rent] a house
租房

buy[purchase] a house
買房

move
搬家
move in / out
搬進 / 搬走

get[take out] a loan
得到貸款
get[take out] a mortgage(loan)
取得抵押貸款

real estate agency
不動產仲介營業處
real estate agent
不動產仲介業者

SENTENCES TO USE

我最近週末都去看房子。	These days, I go house hunting every weekend.
她拿到銀行貸款買了房子。	She took out a loan from a bank and bought a house.
不動產仲介推薦了幾間房子給我。	The real estate agent recommended me several houses.
他住在套房。	He lives in a studio.
那間公寓附有完整的家具。	The apartment is fully furnished.
你的租客已經好幾個月沒付房租了？	Your tenant hasn't paid the monthly rent for months?

townhouse
聯排式住宅

mansion
大廈

apartment
公寓

---

studio 套房
furnished 配有家具的 (↔ **unfurnished**)
rented house 出租房
deposit 保證金
rent 房租（**monthly rent** 月租）
landlord, landlady 屋主、租賃者
tenant, renter 房客、承租人

住家內部、外部

住家外部

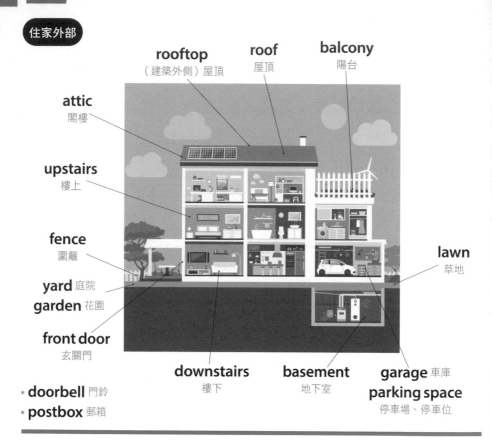

rooftop （建築外側）屋頂
roof 屋頂
balcony 陽台
attic 閣樓
upstairs 樓上
fence 圍籬
yard 庭院
garden 花園
front door 玄關門
lawn 草地
downstairs 樓下
basement 地下室
garage 車庫
parking space 停車場、停車位

* **doorbell** 門鈴
* **postbox** 郵箱

SENTENCES TO USE

我們在屋頂種很多植物。	We grow a lot of plants on our rooftop.
我不考慮沒有陽台的房子。	I don't consider a house without a balcony.
我的房間在樓上。	My room is on the upstairs.
住在有花園的房子是我媽媽的夢想。	My mom's dream is to live in a house with a garden.
那間房子有停車位。	The house has a parking space.
我在地下室放了各種東西。	I keep a lot of things in the basement.

住家內部

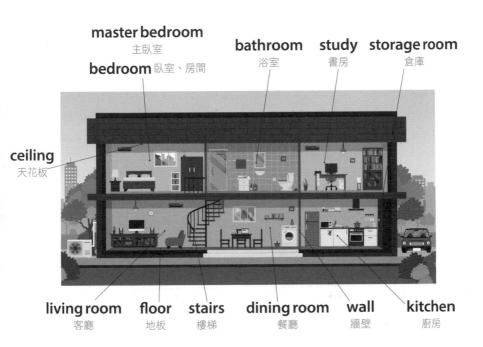

master bedroom
主臥室
bedroom 臥室、房間
bathroom 浴室
study 書房
storage room 倉庫
ceiling 天花板

living room 客廳　**floor** 地板　**stairs** 樓梯　**dining room** 餐廳　**wall** 牆壁　**kitchen** 廚房

SENTENCES TO USE

那間房子有幾間房間？	How many bedrooms does the house have?
他們每天晚上一起聚在客廳看電視。	They get together in the living room and watch TV every evening.
廚房有兩台冰箱。	There are two refrigerators in the kitchen.
我們浴室沒有浴缸。	We don't have a bathtub in our bathroom.
我在天花板貼了很多星星貼紙。	I put a lot of star-shaped stickers on the ceiling.
我每天拖地板。	I mop the floor every day.

家具

wardrobe
衣櫃

built-in wardrobe, closet
嵌入式衣櫃、壁櫥

dresser, chest of drawers
抽屜櫃

dressing table
化妝台

bed
床

bedside table
床邊桌

couch, sofa
沙發

bookcase
書櫃

(dining) table
餐桌

shoe closet, shoe shelf
鞋櫃、鞋架

* 浴室設備
toilet 馬桶
bathtub 浴缸
shower 蓮蓬頭

SENTENCES TO USE

新公寓有嵌入式衣櫃。	The new apartment has a built-in wardrobe.
我應該再買一個抽屜櫃。	I need to buy another chest of drawers.
這張沙發真的很舒服。	This sofa is really comfortable!
雖然有三個書櫃，但還是放不下我的書。	There are three bookcases, but they're not enough for my books.
你自己做鞋櫃嗎？	Did you make your own shoe closet?
我的浴室裡有小浴缸。	There's a small bathtub in my bathroom.

dresser vs. chest of drawers
兩的字都是指抽屜櫃，不過 dresser 通常在抽屜上方有鏡子，drawer 則單指一個抽屜。抽屜櫃是 chest of drawers。

家電用品

light
燈、電燈

television
電視

vacuum cleaner
吸塵器
robot vacuum cleaner 掃地機器人

air conditioner
空調

electric fan
電風扇

desktop computer
桌上型電腦

laptop (computer)
筆記型電腦

washing machine
洗衣機

dryer
（衣服）烘乾機

SENTENCES TO USE

你為什麼不開燈讀書？

Why don't you turn on the light and read a book?

現在的空調不像以前一樣耗電。

Today's air conditioners don't use as much electricity as they used to.

這台筆記型電腦已經出廠五年了。

This laptop is five years old.

最節省家事時間的是洗衣機。

It's the washing machine that cut the housework time the most.

---

top loading vs. front loading
洗衣機有分滾筒式和直立式兩種，用英文該怎麼說呢？直立式洗衣機從上方放置洗滌衣物，因此稱作 **top loading washing machine**。另一方面，滾筒式洗衣機從前方放置洗滌衣物，因此稱作 **front loading washing machine**，很有趣吧？

iron
熨斗

outlet
插座

sewing machine
裁縫機

hair dryer
吹風機

remote control
遙控器

electric razor
電動刮鬍刀

humidifier
加濕器

dehumidifier
除濕機

air cleaner, air purifier
空氣清淨機

radiator
暖房裝置、散熱器

SENTENCES TO USE

冬天太過乾燥，我必須要開加濕器。　It's so dry in winter that I have to turn on the humidifier.

現在有很多家庭有空氣清淨機。　These days, there are many houses with an air cleaner.

turn on / off ~ 開 / 關
家電產品的「開」是 turn on ~，「關」是 turn off ~。

Let's turn on the air conditioner. It's so hot in here.
開空調吧，這裡太熱了。
I think you can turn off the air purifier now.
我覺得你現在可以關掉空氣清淨機。

廚房用品、家電

kitchen cabinet
餐廚櫃

sink 洗手台

refrigerator
冰箱

freezer
冷凍庫、冷凍櫃

kitchen stove, gas stove
瓦斯爐

induction stove, induction cooktop
電磁爐

oven
烤箱

kitchen hood, range hood
抽油煙機

microwave
微波爐

electric rice cooker
電子鍋

dishwasher
洗碗機

toaster
烤吐司機

coffee maker
咖啡機

blender
攪拌機

electric kettle
電熱水壺

water purifier
濾淨飲水機

trash can
垃圾桶

SENTENCES TO USE

我最近在家裡裝了電磁爐。	I recently installed an induction stove at my house.
韓國使用洗碗機的家庭持續增加。	More and more homes are using dishwashers in Korea.
我朋友送我咖啡機當生日禮物。	A friend of mine gave me a coffee maker for my birthday.

water dispenser vs. water purifier
辦公室或公家機關常飲用桶裝水，整個水桶放上機器，可以按出冷水和溫水，那台機器就稱為「飲水機」，英文是 water dispenser；能夠過濾自來水再給水的飲水機，英文是 water purifier。

remodel[renovate] the house
改造（整修）房子

repair the house
修繕房子（修理有問題的地方）

paint the house / a room
油漆房子 / 房間

unblock[clear, unclog] the drain[sewer]
通排水管、下水道

change a light bulb
換燈泡

decorate[redecorate] the interior of ~（重新）裝潢～
repaper the walls 換壁紙
redo the floors 重舖地板
repaint the cabinets 重漆櫥櫃
unclog the toilet 通阻塞的馬桶

SENTENCES TO USE

改造房子花了我們兩個月時間。	It took us two months to renovate the house.
我打給水電工請他處理阻塞的排水管。	I called a plumber and had him unblock the drain.
你不會自己換電燈泡嗎？	Can't you change the light bulb yourself?
我花很多錢裝潢房子。	I spent a lot of money decorating the interior of my house.
你搬家時只要換新壁紙就可以了。	All you have to do for the house when you move in is to repaper the walls.
我們應該要重舖地板。	I think we need to redo the floor.

清潔、打掃用品

vacuum cleaner 吸塵器

cleanser （打掃）清潔劑

mop 拖把

rag 抹布

broom 掃把

dustpan 畚箕

garbage bag 垃圾袋

trash can 垃圾桶

washing machine 洗衣機

dryer （衣服）烘乾機

laundry basket 洗衣籃

laundry detergent 洗衣精、洗衣粉

fabric[fiber] softener 衣物柔軟劑

clothespin 曬衣夾

drying rack 晾衣架

SENTENCES TO USE

吸塵器故障了。	The vacuum cleaner is broken.
你應該用拖把好好擦地板。	You should wipe the floor well with a mop.
用抹布擦一下窗台。	Wipe the windowsill with a rag.
你一定要使用規定的垃圾袋。	You must use a standard plastic garbage bag.
我一定要使用衣物柔軟劑嗎？	Do I have to use fabric softener?
我將衣服晾到晾衣架上。	I hang clothes on a drying rack.

CHAPTER

人際關係

—

Relationship

各種人際關係

家譜、族譜

family tree

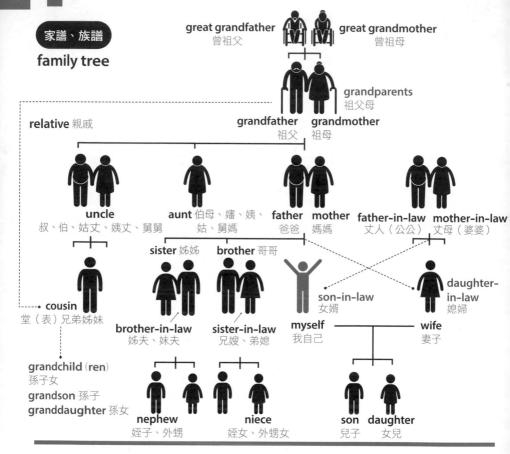

great grandfather 曾祖父　**great grandmother** 曾祖母

grandparents 祖父母

relative 親戚

grandfather 祖父　**grandmother** 祖母

uncle 叔、伯、姑丈、姨丈、舅舅　**aunt** 伯母、嬸、姨、姑、舅媽　**father** 爸爸　**mother** 媽媽　**father-in-law** 丈人（公公）　**mother-in-law** 丈母（婆婆）

sister 姊姊　**brother** 哥哥

cousin 堂（表）兄弟姊妹

son-in-law 女婿　**daughter-in-law** 媳婦

brother-in-law 姊夫、妹夫　**sister-in-law** 兄嫂、弟媳　**myself** 我自己　**wife** 妻子

grandchild (ren) 孫子女
grandson 孫子
granddaughter 孫女

nephew 姪子、外甥　**niece** 姪女、外甥女　**son** 兒子　**daughter** 女兒

SENTENCES TO USE

他的曾祖父參加過獨立運動。

His great grandfather took part in the independence movement.

我的姪子現在是大學生。

My niece is a college student.

雖然我婆婆已經九十多歲了，但她很健康。

My mother-in-law is in her 90s, but she is very healthy.

他是我繼父，但像我爸爸一樣好。

He is my stepfather, but he is as good as a real father.

她是我的同事。

She is my coworker.

他和我只是同學而已。

He and I are just schoolmates.

stepmother
新媽、繼母

stepsister
異父或異母姊妹

stepfather
新爸、繼父

stepbrother
異父或異母兄弟

single parent 單親
（**single father** 單親父親, **single mother** 單親母親）

* **sibling** 兄弟姊妹
* **twins** 雙胞胎
* **triplets** 三胞胎

friend, buddy 朋友
acquaintance 認識的人
colleague, coworker 同事
schoolmate 同校同學
classmate 同班同學
roommate 室友
partner 事業夥伴、愛人

in-laws
in-laws 姻親關係。因為結婚而成為法律上的親戚，所以稱為
in-laws。親家、婆家、岳家都可以稱為 in-laws。

colleague vs. coworker
colleague 和 coworker 都是「同事」的意思，但兩者有所差異。colleague 指的
是同職業的人，尤其是從事相同專業職位的人，coworker 則是指在公司內職等相
似的人。

2 交際、關係

introduce 介紹
get to know 得知、認識
get acquainted with 和某人熟識、變熟
make friends with, get to be friends with 和某人結交
get along with, get on well with, be on good terms with
和某人好好相處、關係良好
hang out with 和某人出去玩、閒晃
be sociable, be outgoing 很會社交的
be shy, be shy of strangers 認生的
visit, call on 拜訪
have good manners 有禮貌
have no manners 沒禮貌

SENTENCES TO USE

我在倫敦認識他。	I got to know him in London.
他們在國中時熟識。	They made friends with each other when they were in middle school.
宇振和大家相處得很好。	Woojin gets along well with people.
智宇很會社交。	Jiyu is very sociable.
我很怕生。	I'm shy of strangers.
他非常沒禮貌。	He really has no manners.

fall out with 和某人關係變差
talk about someone behind one's back 在背後談論某人
argue with, have an argument with 和某人爭論
quarrel with 和某人爭吵
fight with 和某人打架

---

make up with, reconcile with 和某人和解

SENTENCES TO USE

你和他關係變差嗎？	Did you fall out with him?
我不喜歡和別人吵架。	I don't like to argue with people.
你們還沒和好嗎？	Have you guys made up yet?

argue, quarrel, fight
argue、quarrel、fight 基本上都是「吵架」的意思，不過三個單字有所差異。

- argue：表示「爭論」的意思，用言語來爭論某事時。
- quarrel：用來指比 argue 更激烈的爭吵，也就是言語上的爭執。
- fight：指包含身體暴力的吵架。

相親

have[go on] a blind date 相親
have a crush on 愛上某人
fall in love with 和某人陷入愛河
fall in love at first sight with 對某人一見鍾情
ask someone out (on a date) 對某人提出約會邀約
have a date with 和某人約會
see, date, go out with 和某人約會、交往
be in a relationship 談戀愛中
be in a romantic relationship with 和某人交往、戀愛
break up with（原本交往的關係）和某人分手

SENTENCES TO USE

他每個週末都去相親。　　　　　He has a blind date every weekend.

欣蒂一定是愛上那個男人。　　　Cindy must have a crush on the man.

兩個人彼此一見鍾情。　　　　　The two fell in love at first sight.

你約她了嗎？　　　　　　　　　Did you ask her out?

你有正在交往的人嗎？　　　　　Are you seeing anyone?

聽說他們兩個分手了。　　　　　They say the two of them broke up.

結婚、別離

propose to
向某人求婚

get engaged to
和某人訂婚

bride
新娘

get married to
和某人結婚

groom, bridegroom
新郎

engagement 訂婚
fiancé 未婚夫 / **fiancée** 未婚妻
wedding 結婚典禮
love marriage 戀愛結婚
arranged marriage 包辦婚姻
matchmaker 媒人
be married 已婚

SENTENCES TO USE

我向男朋友求婚。	I proposed to my boyfriend.
新郎十分緊張。	The groom is very nervous.
我十二年前結婚。	I got married 12 years ago.
他是我的未婚夫。	He is my fiancé.
我想要省略結婚典禮。	I'd like to skip the wedding.
你是戀愛結婚還是包辦婚姻？	Did you have a love marriage or an arranged marriage?

hold a wedding reception
舉辦婚宴

go on one's honeymoon
去蜜月旅行

go to ~ for one's honeymoon
去 ～ 蜜月旅行

have an affair with
和某人有染

cheat on
瞞著某人外遇

get divorced
離婚

divorce
離婚

---

lose one's wife / husband, be widowed 妻子 / 丈夫過世
widow 寡婦
widower 鰥夫

不婚

be single, be unmarried, be not married 單身（不婚）
live single [unmarried] 過單身（不婚）生活
remain single [unmarried] 維持單身（不婚）

SENTENCES TO USE

蜜月旅行我想去南法。	I'd like to go to southern France for my honeymoon.
男方外遇了嗎？	Did the man cheat on her?
那位演員又離婚了。	The actress got divorced again.
她五年前因為事故失去了丈夫。	She lost her husband in an accident five years ago.
我不婚。	I am single.
你要一輩子單身嗎？	Are you going to live unmarried for the rest of your life?

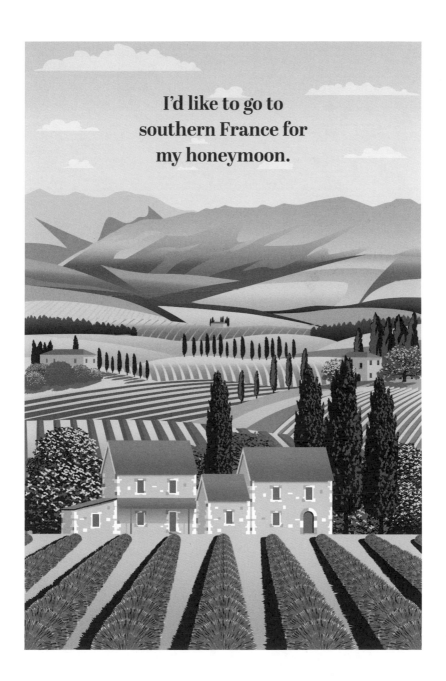

I'd like to go to
southern France for
my honeymoon.

CHAPTER

健康

———

Health

生理現象

pulse
脈搏、脈搏跳動

one's heart beats 心臟跳動
heart beat 心搏
heart rate 心率

breathe 呼吸
breath 呼吸、氣息

shiver
顫抖

sweat
汗、流汗

bleed 流血
blood 血

blood pressure
血壓

blood sugar
血糖

SENTENCES TO USE

那位醫生測量患者的脈搏。 | The doctor measured the patient's pulse.

他的心跳一分鐘不到50。 | His heart rate is less than 50 beats per minute.

因為微細粉塵而難以呼吸。 | It was hard to breathe because of the fine dust.

那位男子吃熱食時流了很多汗。 | The man sweats a lot when he eats hot food.

請問血壓多少正常？ | What's the normal blood pressure?

如果你空腹時血糖超過140，那就是糖尿病。 | If your fasting blood sugar is over 140, you're diabetic.

digest 消化（**digestion** 消化）
absorb 吸收（**absorption** 吸收）
secrete 分泌（**secretion** 分泌、分泌物）
go to the bathroom〔toilet〕, relieve oneself〔nature〕, do one's needs
去化妝室、大小便

pee, take a pee
小便
urine, pee 小便

**move one's bowels,
poop, defecate** 大便
poop, feces, excrement 大便

fart, break wind
放屁
hold in (one's) fart
把屁憋著

burp
打嗝
hold in a burp
忍住打嗝

vomit, throw up
嘔吐

SENTENCES TO USE

胃、腸等器官負責消化。 The stomach, intestines and other organs are responsible for digestion.

催產素由腦下垂體分泌。 Oxytocin is secreted by the pituitary gland.

我急著去化妝室。 I'm in a hurry to go to the bathroom.

我在外面無法上大號。 I can't poop outside my house.

我無法忍耐不放屁。 I couldn't hold in my fart.

你應該在大家面前忍住打嗝。 You have to hold in a burp in front of people.

nutrition
營養、營養學、食物

carbohydrate
碳水化合物

protein
蛋白質

fat
脂肪

saturated fat
飽和脂肪

unsaturated fat
不飽和脂肪

dietary fiber
膳食纖維

cholesterol
膽固醇

vitamin 維他命
mineral 礦物質
iron 鐵質
sugar 糖
nutritious 營養價值高的
nutrient 營養素、營養成分
essential nutrient 必需營養素

SENTENCES TO USE

我吃太多碳水化合物，應該稍微減量。

I eat too many carbohydrates. I need to cut down on them a little.

蛋白質分為動物性和植物性。

There are animal protein and vegetable protein.

飽和脂肪對身體不好，你不該吃太多。

Saturated fat is bad for your body, so you shouldn't eat it too much.

很多人透過保健食品攝取維他命和礦物質。

Many people take vitamins and minerals through supplements.

你應該要吃美味又具營養價值的食物。

You should eat tasty and nutritious foods.

必需營養素有什麼？

What are the essential nutrients?

cut down on 減少～
processed food 加工食品
high in ～高的
low in ～低的
calorie-controlled diet 熱量控制飲食
balanced diet 均衡飲食
vegetarian 素食主義者
overeat 過食
go on a diet 開始減重
be on a diet 減重中
fast 禁食
skip a meal 不吃飯、少吃　餐

SENTENCES TO USE

我們應該少吃鹹和油膩的食物。	We have to cut down on salty and greasy food.
牡蠣中含有大量鐵質。	Oysters are high in iron.
均衡飲食非常重要。	It's important to have a balanced diet.
他們說那位歌手是素食主義者。	They say the singer is a vegetarian.
她是不是一整年都在減重？	Isn't she on a diet all year long?
斷食對身體好還是不好呢？	Would fasting be good for your body or not?

work out, exercise
運動

warm up
做暖身運動
stretch 伸展

jog 慢跑
run 跑步

go to the gym
上健身房

go swimming
去游泳

do aerobics
做有氧運動

do weight training
做重訓

do squats
做深蹲

do sit-ups
做仰臥起坐

do push-ups
做伏地挺身

do circuit training
做循環訓練

SENTENCES TO USE

為了你的健康請運動。	Please exercise for your health.
請在工作的空檔做伸展。	Stretch while you work.
我一週去健身房三次。	I go to the gym three times a week.
我們應該從中年開始做重訓。	From middle age, we should do weight training.
我每天做深蹲。	I do squats every day.
你可以做幾下伏地挺身？	How many push-ups can you do?

jump rope
跳繩

do[practice] yoga
做瑜珈

do Pilates
做皮拉提斯

meditate
冥想

get a massage
（被）按摩

watch one's weight 控制體重
lose weight 降低體重、減重、減肥
gain weight 增加體重、增重、增肥
stop[quit] smoking 戒菸
stop[quit] drinking 戒酒

SENTENCES TO USE

她做瑜珈十年了。	She's been doing yoga for 10 years.
我必須減重，大約五公斤。	I have to lose weight. About 5 kilograms.
他在癌症手術後戒了菸和酒。	He quit smoking and drinking after cancer surgery.

gym 健身房
- personal trainer, fitness instructor：健身教練
- hire a personal trainer：聘請私人教練
- treadmill：跑步機
- weight：槓鈴
- exercise bike：健身腳踏車
- rowing machine：划船機

4 疾病、受傷

ache（身體、頭、心等）疼痛
hurt, be painful（某部位）疼痛
have pain in ～ 痛

be sick, be ill
不舒服、生病的

have a fever
發燒

have〔feel〕a chill
發冷

feel dizzy
暈眩

bleed
流血

be itchy
癢的

be sore
（發炎或傷口）痛、痠痛

be swollen
腫的

vomit, throw up
嘔吐

SENTENCES TO USE

我運動太久，身體很痠痛。	I exercised for a long time, and I ache all over.
我膝蓋很痛，沒辦法走太久。	My knee is so painful I cannot walk long.
我發燒也發冷。	I have a fever and a chill.
我的眼睛又癢又充血。	My eyes are itchy and bloodshot.
我今天站好幾個小時，腿都腫了。	My legs are swollen since I've been standing for hours today.
他把吃的東西都吐了出來。	He threw up everything he ate.

have a headache 頭痛　**have a backache** 腰痛　**have a stomachache** 肚子痛　**catch[have] a cold** 感冒

have a flu 得流感　**have a runny nose** 流鼻水　**cough** 咳嗽　**sneeze** 打噴嚏

have a sore throat 喉嚨痛　**have[get] diarrhea, have loose bowels** 腹瀉　**have a bloody nose** 流鼻血　**have an allergy to, be allergic to** 對～過敏

SENTENCES TO USE

我因為頭痛而吃了止痛藥。 — I took a painkiller because I had a headache.

我媽媽腰痛，經常針灸。 — My mom has a backache and often gets acupuncture.

我覺得我每年得一次感冒。 — I think I catch a cold once a year.

我咳嗽、喉嚨痛好幾天了。 — I've been coughing and have had a sore throat for a few days.

我喝牛奶就會拉肚子。 — I have diarrhea whenever I drink milk.

他對雞蛋過敏。 — He's allergic to eggs.

disease 疾病、疾患
chronic disease 慢性疾病
illness, sickness 疾病、生病
disorder（身心機能的）障礙
symptom 症狀
infection 感染、傳染病
germ 細菌
virus 病毒
inflammation 發炎
bleeding 出血
rash 疹子
blister 水泡

SENTENCES TO USE

人類至今仍有許多疾病無法克服。	There still are many diseases that man has not conquered.
自閉症是眾所皆知的發展障礙。	Autism is a well-known developmental disorder.
氣喘的症狀是什麼？	What are the symptoms of asthma?
想要避免感染，最重要的是好好洗手。	It is important to wash your hands thoroughly to prevent infection.
這個藥能退燒和緩解發炎。	This medicine reduces a fever and relieves inflammation.
我因食物中毒而全身起疹子。	I have a rash all over my body from food poisoning.

事故、受傷

get injured, get hurt, be wounded 受傷
have a car accident 出車禍
get hurt from a fall 跌倒受傷
get a bruise 瘀血
get a scar 留疤痕
have(suffer) burns 燒燙傷
get a cut on ～ 被（刀子）劃、割
sprain one's ankle 扭傷腳踝
wear a cast 打石膏

SENTENCES TO USE

我的一位朋友騎腳踏車時受傷。	A friend of mine got hurt while riding a bike.
他因車禍而住院。	He was hospitalized in a car accident.
我跌倒然後腿瘀血。	I fell and got a bruise on my leg.
他小時候被燙傷過。	He suffered burns when he was a child.
我做菜時割到手指頭。	I got a cut on my finger while I was cooking.
智秀扭傷腳踝並打了石膏。	Jisu sprained her ankle and wore a cast.

各種疾病

addiction 成癮	**alcoholism** 酒精中毒
anemia 貧血	**angina** 心絞痛
appendicitis 盲腸炎	**arrhythmia, an irregular pulse** 心律不整
arthritis 關節炎	**asthma** 氣喘
atopy 異位性皮膚炎	**benign tumor** 良性腫瘤
brain tumor 腦腫瘤	**cancer** 癌症
cavity 蛀牙	**cold** 感冒
constipation 便祕	**dementia** 失智症
depression 憂鬱症	**diabetes** 糖尿病
enteritis 腸炎	**food poisoning** 食物中毒
gastritis 胃炎	**heart attack** 心臟病發作、心臟麻痺
heart disease 心臟病	**hemorrhoids, piles** 痔瘡
high blood pressure 高血壓	**hyperlipidemia** 高脂血症
indigestion 消化不良	**influenza, flu** 流感
insomnia 失眠	**leukemia** 白血病
malignant tumor 惡性腫瘤	**measles** 麻疹
mental disorder 精神障礙	**mental illness** 精神疾病
migraine 偏頭痛	**myocardial infarction** 心肌梗塞
osteoporosis 骨質疏鬆症	**panic disorder** 恐慌症
periodontitis 牙周病	**pneumonia** 肺炎
shingles, herpes zoster 帶狀皰疹	**slipped disc** 椎間盤突出
stomach ulcer 胃潰瘍	**stroke** 中風
tonsillitis 扁桃體炎	**tuberculosis** 肺結核

057

癌症

brain cancer 腦癌
laryngeal cancer 喉癌
oral cancer 口腔癌
tongue cancer 舌癌
thyroid cancer 甲狀腺癌
esophagus cancer 食道癌
lung cancer 肺癌
breast cancer 乳癌
stomach cancer, gastric cancer 胃癌
liver cancer 肝癌
gallbladder cancer 膽囊癌
renal cancer 腎癌
pancreatic cancer 胰腺癌
uterine cancer 子宮癌
ovarian cancer 卵巢癌
prostate cancer 攝護腺癌
colorectal cancer 大腸癌
rectal cancer 直腸癌
acute myeloid leukemia 急性骨髓性白血病
blood cancer 血癌
skin cancer 皮膚癌

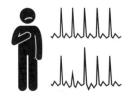

醫院、治療、藥物

醫院、治療

**go to the doctor,
go see a doctor**
去醫院、給醫生診療
examine 檢查、診療

**be treated, get
treatment**
接受治療

heal from
治癒、好轉
recover from
從 ～ 恢復

**have(get) a shot
(an injection)**
被打針

**be prescribed
medicine**
被開藥

get an IV
吊點滴

have(take) a blood test 接受血液檢查
have(take) a urine test 接受尿液檢查

SENTENCES TO USE

你咳嗽好幾天了，你應該去看醫生。	You've been coughing for days. You should go see a doctor.
他因為慢性病而長期接受治療。	He has been treated for a long time because of a chronic disease.
那個傷口花了好幾週才痊癒。	It took several weeks for the wound to heal.
如果你去醫院打針，馬上就會好起來。	If you go to the hospital and get a shot, you'll be well soon.
我偏頭痛，醫院開了藥給我。	I was prescribed medicine at the hospital for migraine.
我做了血液和尿液檢查。	I had a blood test and a urine test.

have[take, get] an X-ray
拍 X 光

do a CT scan
做電腦斷層掃描 (CT)
do an MRI
做磁振造影檢查 (MRI)

have physical therapy
做物理治療

have surgery [an operation]
接受手術

get[have, take] a medical check-up[medical examination]
做健康檢查

enter a hospital, be hospitalized 住院
leave a hospital 出院

SENTENCES TO USE

你有拍過胸部 X 光嗎？	Have you ever had a chest X-ray?
她做了心臟瓣膜手術。	She had heart valve surgery.
我每兩年做一次健康檢查。	I get a medical check-up every second year.

各種科別

internal medicine 內科
pediatrics 小兒科
neurology 神經內科
psychiatry 精神科
orthopedics 骨科
ophthalmology 眼科
dental clinic, dentist's 牙科

surgery 外科
obstetrics 產科, gynecology 婦科
neurosurgery 神經外科
dermatology 皮膚科
plastic surgery 整形外科
otolaryngology 耳鼻喉科
oriental medical clinic 中醫診所

hospital 醫院
clinic 診所
physician 內科醫生
surgeon 外科醫生
patient 患者
ambulance 救護車
stethoscope 聽診器
thermometer 體溫計
ER (emergency room) 急診室
ICU (intensive care unit) 加護病房
doctor's office, examining room 診療室
operating room 手術室
patient's room 病房
sick ward 住院病房

SENTENCES TO USE

請問這附近有牙醫嗎？	Is there a dental clinic nearby?
外科醫生是動手術的醫生。	Surgeons are doctors who perform surgeries.
每五分鐘就有救護車載急診病患來。	Every five minutes an ambulance came with an emergency patient.
家裡最好有一個體溫計。	You'd better have a thermometer in the house.
我的鄰居昨晚被載去急診。	Last night, my neighbor was taken to the emergency room.
請問加護病房可以探病嗎？	Can I see a patient in the intensive care unit?

藥物

take medicine 吃藥
prescribe a drug 開處方藥
pill, tablet 藥丸
liquid medicine 藥水
powder, powdered medicine 藥粉
ointment 軟膏
painkiller 止痛藥
fever reducer 退燒藥
digestive medicine 消化藥
antiseptic 消毒藥劑
pain relief patch 止痛貼布
eye drop 眼藥水
sleeping pill 安眠藥

SENTENCES TO USE

如果你不舒服就別忍耐，要去吃藥。	When you are sick, don't hold back and do take medicine.
小孩子不太會吃藥粉。	Young children have difficulty taking powdered medicine.
止痛藥和退燒藥是家庭常備藥。	Painkillers and fever reducers are household medicines.
我沒吃安眠藥就睡不著。	I can't sleep without sleeping pills.

first aid kit 急救箱
adhesive bandage OK 繃   **bandage** 繃帶
cotton pad 化妝棉、棉布   **band-aid** 邦迪牌 OK 繃、OK 繃
antiseptic 消毒藥劑   **ice pack** 冰敷袋
fever reducer 退燒藥   **painkiller** 止痛藥
ointment 軟膏

UNIT 6 死亡

die 死亡
pass away 過世
condole with somebody on the death of 向～哀悼～的過世
offer one's sympathy for the loss of 對 ～ 表示哀悼
Please accept my sympathy for 我對 ～ 表示慰問
the dead[deceased] 故人、亡者
corpse 遺體
commit suicide, kill oneself 自我了結生命
be brain-dead 腦死狀態

funeral 葬禮
funeral hall 殯儀館

SENTENCES TO USE

我祖父過世了。	My grandfather passed away.
我對您母親的逝世深表哀悼。	Please accept my sympathy for the loss of your mother.
逝者是我國中的老師。	The deceased is my middle school teacher.
那位小說家自我了結生命。	The novelist committed suicide.
他因為車禍而陷入腦死狀態。	He was brain-dead in a car accident.
那位政治人物的葬禮有非常多人參加。	Numerous people attended the politician's funeral.

coffin
棺材

bury 埋葬
burial 埋葬

grave, tomb
墳墓、墓
cemetery 墓地

shroud 壽衣
cremate the body 火葬遺體（**cremation** 火葬）
natural burial 自然葬
cinerarium 骨灰罈

SENTENCES TO USE

過去韓國會實行土葬。	In the past, the body was buried in Korea.
怎麼樣的人會埋葬在公墓？	What kind of people are buried in the National Cemetery?
韓國的壽衣主要以絲、棉或麻製成。	In Korea, a shroud is usually made of silk, cotton, or hemp cloth.
最近遺體主要以火葬處理。	These days, bodies are usually cremated.
近來有越來越多人選擇自然葬。	These days, more and more people choose natural burial.
我每隔幾個月去看一次父母的骨灰罈。	I visit the cinerarium where my parents are every few months.

CHAPTER

休閒與興趣

Leisure & Hobbies

各種休閒

be on vacation 度假中 / **go on vacation** 度假

go camping 去露營

go on[have] a picnic 去野餐

go to[visit] a museum / **(an art) gallery** 參觀博物館 / 美術館

go to an amusement park / **a theme park** 去遊樂園 / 主題樂園

go hiking 去健行

go fishing 去釣魚

work out, exercise 運動

go to the gym 上健身房 / **work out at the gym** 在健身房運動

ride a bicycle[bike] 騎腳踏車

SENTENCES TO USE

你今年夏天什麼時候會去度假？

When will you go on vacation this summer?

我常常帶著我的狗去野餐。

I often go on picnics with my dogs.

他一有時間就去美術館。

He goes to the art gallery whenever he has time.

找時間一起去健行。

Let's go hiking together sometime.

我空閒時去健身房運動。

I work out at the gym in my spare time.

我喜歡沿著河道騎腳踏車。

I like riding a bike along the river.

do[practice] yoga 做瑜伽
take a walk, go for a walk 散步
read a book 看書
join a book club 參加讀書會
listen to music 聽音樂
go to a concert 去演唱會
watch TV 看電視
watch a movie 看電影
go to the movies 去看電影
watch[see] a play / **a musical** / **an opera** 看戲劇 / 音樂劇 / 歌劇
play the piano / **drums** / **guitar** 彈鋼琴 / 打鼓 / 彈吉他

SENTENCES TO USE

自從搬來鄉下，我每天早上都去散步。	I take a walk every morning since I moved to the country.
知祐喜歡看書，所以她也加入讀書會。	Jiho likes reading books, so she also joined a book club.
我在2018年春天去了 Coldplay 在韓國的演唱會。	I went to Coldplay's concert in Korea in the spring of 2018.
週末時，我會去看電影或在家看電視。	On weekends, I go to the movies or watch TV at home.
我的興趣？看音樂劇。	My hobby? Watching musicals.
我每週打鼓一次。	I play the drums once a week.

take pictures 照相
draw, paint 繪畫
make ~ by hand 手作 ～
make models 做模型
knit 編織
cook 料理
bake bread / **cookies** 烤麵包 / 餅乾
do gardening 做園藝
arrange flowers 插花
keep[raise] a pet 養寵物

SENTENCES TO USE

畫畫讓我感到放鬆。	Painting makes me feel at ease.
他喜歡自己用木頭製作一些物品。	He enjoys making things by hand out of wood.
我織了一條厚圍巾並送給祖母當禮物。	I knitted a muffler and gifted it to my grandmother.
我最近的興趣是烤麵包。	My hobby these days is baking bread.
聽說很多英國人把園藝當興趣。	They say many British people do gardening as a hobby.
那家人養了兩隻狗和三隻貓。	The family keeps two dogs and three cats.

use social media[SNS] 使用社群媒體

watch YouTube videos 觀看 YouTube 影片

write a blog post 寫部落格文章

learn a foreign language 學習外國語

play mobile games 玩手遊（手機遊戲）

play board games 玩桌遊（桌上遊戲）

play cards 玩撲克牌

sing in a karaoke box 去 KTV 包廂唱歌

go to a club 去俱樂部、社團

go to a party 去派對

SENTENCES TO USE

我覺得我下班後會花幾個小時在社群媒體上。	I think I use social media for a few hours after work.
最近的小孩常常在 YouTube 上看影片。	Kids watch YouTube videos a lot these days.
我每天至少在部落格發一篇文。	I write a blog post at least once every day.
他退休後學習外語當興趣。	He's learning a foreign language as a hobby after retirement.
你要一整天都玩手機遊戲嗎？	Are you just going to play mobile games all day?
如果你去KTV包廂唱歌，可以釋放壓力。	If you sing in a karaoke box, you relieve your stress.

take[go on] a trip, travel 去旅行
take[go on] a one-day trip 去一日遊（**one-day trip, day trip** 一日遊 ）
go on a package tour 跟套裝行程
go sightseeing 去觀光
travel domestically 在國內旅行 / **domestic travel[trip]** 國內旅行
have[go on] a guided tour 跟導覽行程
travel alone 獨自旅行
go on a school trip[an excursion] 去校外教學

go backpacking,
go on a backpacking trip
背包旅行

travel abroad,
go on an overseas trip
出國旅行
overseas travel[trip] 國外旅行

SENTENCES TO USE

我媽媽喜歡跟套裝行程。	My mom prefers to go on a package tour.
我常常在國內旅行。每個月我四處去走走。	I often travel domestically. I go anywhere every month.
我們在梵蒂岡有導覽行程。	We had a guided tour of the Vatican.
我高中時去慶州校外教學。	I went on a school trip to Gyeongju when I was in high school.
秀敏去南美洲背包旅行。	Sumin went on a backpacking trip to South America.
最近很多人出國旅行。	A lot of people travel abroad these days.

travel by train / **car** / **bus** / **plane** 搭火車 / 汽車 / 公車 / 飛機去旅行
pack one's bags for the trip 打包行李
(**travel**) **itinerary** 行程
festival 慶典
souvenir 紀念品

---

go on a cruise
搭郵輪旅行

tourist attraction
觀光景點

historic site
歷史遺跡

ancient palace
古代宮殿

exchange money 換外幣
money exchange 外幣兌換

tour guide
導遊

SENTENCES TO USE

我搭火車遊覽整個義大利。	I traveled all over Italy by train.
你旅行的行李打包了嗎？	Have you packed your bags for the trip?
你規劃好阿拉斯加的行程了嗎？	Did you make your itinerary for Alaska?
香港主要觀光景點都在哪裡？	Where are the major tourist attractions in Hong Kong?
首爾有很多古代宮殿。	There are many ancient palaces in Seoul.
你去哪裡換外幣？	Where did you exchange money?

機場、飛機

passport 護照
suitcase 行李箱
baggage 行李
e-ticket 電子機票
boarding pass 登機證
one-way ticket 單程機票
round-trip ticket 來回機票
direct[nonstop] flight 直達班機
check-in counter 報到櫃檯
check in baggage 託運行李
check-in baggage 託運的行李
carry-on bag 手提行李
go through passport control 通過入境審查
have a security check 過安全檢查
duty-free shop 免稅店
get ~ tax-free[duty-free] 免稅購買 ~
departure gate 登機口
get on[board] a plane 登機
economy / **business** / **first class** 經濟 / 商務 / 頭等艙
in-flight service 機上服務
window seat 靠窗位置
aisle seat 靠走道位置
land at the airport 在機場降落
baggage claim 行李提領區
declare 報關
customs 海關
jet-lag 時差

住宿

hotel 飯店
hostel 旅館
guesthouse 廉價旅館、民宿
B&B (bed and breakfast) 附早餐的民宿
air B&B 愛彼迎
villa 度假別墅
resort 度假勝地
motel 汽車旅館
front desk 櫃檯
receptionist 接待人員
room with a view 景觀房
vacancies 空房
complimentary shuttle 免費接駁巴士
make a reservation 預訂
stay in a hotel 住在飯店
check in 辦理入住
check out 辦理退房

3 電影、戲劇、音樂劇

電影

movie theater 電影院
multiplex 影城
box office 售票處、票房
audience 觀眾
director 電影導演
film crew 電影製作團隊
movie star 電影明星（**actor, actress** 電影、戲劇、音樂劇演員）
cast 卡司、出演者
main character 主角
supporting role 配角
hero / heroine 男主角 / 女主角
villain 反派
special effects 特效
stunt man / woman 特技替身演員
screenplay, scenario 電影劇本、腳本
line 台詞

SENTENCES TO USE

那部電影擁有超讚的成功票房。	The movie was a huge box-office success.
那部電影吸引了一千萬觀眾。	The movie attracted 10 million audiences.
配角們非常有魅力。	Supporting roles were very attractive.
有很多印象深刻的台詞。	There were many memorable lines.

電影種類

drama 劇情片
comedy 喜劇
action movie 動作片
thriller 驚悚片
animation 動畫

period[costume] piece 時代劇
romantic comedy 浪漫喜劇
science fiction 科幻片
crime drama 犯罪片

戲劇、音樂劇

play 戲劇、劇本
playwright 劇作家
theater 劇場
stage 舞台
comedy 喜劇
tragedy 悲劇
performance 表演、演技
costumes 服裝
dialogue 劇中對話
monologue 獨白
aside 旁白
act 幕
scene 場
ensemble 音樂劇的合唱團、群舞
get[take] a curtain call 謝幕
give applause 鼓掌
give a standing ovation 起立鼓掌

SENTENCES TO USE

那部劇是愛爾蘭劇作家寫的。	The play was written by an Irish playwright.
那是喜劇還是悲劇？	Is that a comedy or a tragedy?
那部音樂劇的服裝很華麗。	The musical has very fancy costumes.
〈哈姆雷特〉共有5幕。	*Hamlet* consists of five acts.
演員們前去謝幕。	The actors got a curtain call.
觀眾起立鼓掌。	The audience gave a standing ovation.

音樂、演奏會

classical music 古典音樂
pop (ular) song 流行音樂
orchestra 管弦樂團
band 樂團
melody 音樂、旋律
lyrics 歌詞

choir
合唱團、聖歌隊

solo
獨唱、獨奏

musician
音樂家
singer-songwriter
創作歌手

SENTENCES TO USE

我對古典音樂所知不多。	I don't know much about classical music.
熙秀在市立管弦樂團拉小提琴。	Heesoo plays the violin in the city orchestra.
他在一個搖滾樂團裡彈貝斯。	He plays the bass guitar in a rock band.
我喜歡這首歌的歌詞。	I love the lyrics of this song.
我曾是高中合唱團的一員。	I was a member of the high school choir.
英國歌手愛黛兒是一位創作歌手。	British singer Adele is a singer-songwriter.

listen to music 聽音樂

 sing a song 唱歌

 play the ~（樂器）彈奏

 compose 作曲
composer 作曲家

 **conduct** 指揮
conductor 指揮家

 perform 演奏、表演
busk 街頭表演

 **go to a concert** 去演唱會

book[buy] a ticket 訂票、購票
call for an encore 請求安可
give applause 鼓掌
give a standing ovation 起立鼓掌

SENTENCES TO USE

俊彈鋼琴當作興趣。	Jun plays the piano as a hobby.
我們要在學校慶典上表演。	We're going to perform at the school festival.
那個音樂家常常在弘大街頭表演。	The musician often busks in the Hongdae area.
你買到 BTS 演唱會的票了嗎？	Did you manage to book tickets for the BTS concert?
觀眾請求安可。	The audience called for an encore.
他們給歌手大大的鼓掌。	They gave big applause to the singer.

5 書籍

author, writer 作家、作者
title 書名
publish 出版
publisher, publishing company 出版社
editor 編輯
edition 版次
hard cover 精裝
paperback 平裝
plot 情節
character 角色
page-turner 愛不釋手的書

e-book 電子書
e-reader 電子書閱讀器

audio book
有聲書

bookmark
書籤

SENTENCES TO USE

那位作家的新書會在下個月出版。 The author's new book will be published next month.

我終於與出版社簽訂合約！ I finally signed a contract with a publishing company!

我超想要那本書的初版。 I'm dying to get the first edition of the book.

《麥田捕手》的劇情是什麼？ What's the plot of *The Catcher in the Rye*?

小說裡面你最喜歡哪個角色？ Who is your favorite character in the novel?

我還不太習慣電子書。 I'm not used to e-books yet.

067

書籍種類

novel 小說	**essay** 論文、散文、評論
fiction 虛構的事、小說	**non-fiction** 非小說、紀實文學
self-help book 勵志書籍	**fairy tale** 童話
fable 寓言	**collection of poems** 詩集
science-fiction 科幻小說	**crime novel** 犯罪小說
detective novel 偵探小說	**romance** 愛情小說
fantasy 奇幻小說	**biography** 傳記
autobiography 自傳	**travel essay** 旅行散文
encyclopedia 百科全書	**dictionary** 字典
comic (book) 漫畫書	**cookbook** 料理書
travel guidebook 旅遊書	**textbook** 教科書
magazine 雜誌	

newspaper (headline, article, editorial) 報紙（標題、報導、社論）

SENTENCES TO USE

那本書是小說還是紀實？	Is the book fiction or nonfiction?
曾經有段時間勵志書籍賣得很好。	There was a time when self-help books were selling a lot.
海蒂讀很多偵探小說和犯罪小說。	Heidi reads a lot of detective novels and crime novels.

書店

online bookstore 網路書店
second-hand bookstore 二手書店
independent bookstore 獨立書店
large[grand] bookstore 大型書店

6 電視、綜藝

cable TV 有線電視
IPTV (Internet Protocol Television) 網路協定電視
broadcasting station(company) 電視台、電視公司
show 綜藝
episode 集
season 季
host 主持人
weather forecaster 氣象預報員
TV commercial 電視廣告
commercial break 廣告時間
celebrity culture 名人文化
household name 家喻戶曉的人

satellite TV
衛星電視

channel
頻道

(news) anchor
新聞主播

reporter
記者

SENTENCES TO USE

那家電視台專門做紀錄片。	The broadcasting station specializes in documentaries.
我錯過那部劇昨天那集！	I missed yesterday's episode of the drama!
有人不認識那位主持人嗎？	Is there anyone who doesn't know the host?
最近在電視節目中間會出現廣告。	There are TV commercials in the middle of the program these days.
那位新聞主播因為很會訪問而出名。	The news anchor is famous for being very good at interviews.
那位記者為什麼結巴？	Why is that reporter stammering?

068

各種電視節目

news 新聞
documentary 紀錄片
current affairs TV show 時事評論節目
drama 戲劇
soap opera 肥皂劇
sitcom 情境喜劇
comedy 喜劇
period drama 時代劇
talk show 脫口秀
quiz show 益智節目
cartoon 卡通
reality TV show 實境節目
children's show 兒童節目
cooking show 料理節目
shopping channel 購物頻道
talent show 才藝表演、達人秀（展現歌唱、舞蹈等才能）

---

soap opera

soap opera 通常指在白天以家庭主婦為對象播送的電視或廣播連續劇。內容以訴說彼此感情、煽情或是輕鬆的內容為主。soap opera 這個名稱由來是因為早期肥皂業者會在這類戲劇中間插入廣告。

電視相關表達
• turn on the TV：打開電視
• turn off the TV：關上電視
• turn up the volume：提高音量
• turn down the volume：降低音量
• change channels：轉換頻道

7 運動

play ~

soccer 踢足球
basketball 打籃球
volleyball 打排球
table tennis 打桌球

baseball 打棒球
badminton 打網球
tennis 打羽球
golf 打高爾夫

do ~

boxing 打拳擊
gymnastics 做體操
a long jump 跳遠

Taekwondo 打跆拳道
a high jump 跳高
a bungee jump 玩高空彈跳

****run a marathon** 跑馬拉松

SENTENCES TO USE

全世界的男孩子都愛踢足球。	Boys all over the world play soccer a lot.
我高中時常常打籃球。	I used to play basketball often when I was in high school.
你打過桌球嗎？	Have you ever played table tennis?
我的小孩7歲開始打跆拳道。	My child has been doing Taekwondo since he was seven.
給我多少錢，我都不會去高空彈跳。	I can't do a bungee jump no matter how much money I'll be given.
他已超過70歲，仍然去跑馬拉松。	He's over seventy, but he runs a marathon.

go ~
mountain climbing 去爬山
rock climbing 去攀岩
cycling 去騎腳踏車
skating 去溜冰
skateboarding 去滑板
skiing 去滑雪
snowboarding 去滑雪板
horse riding 去騎馬
canoeing 去滑獨木舟
skydiving 去跳傘
paragliding 去玩飛行傘
diving 去潛水
scuba-diving 去水肺潛水
snorkeling 去浮潛

SENTENCES TO USE

南佶說他這週六要去攀岩。

Namgil said he's going to go rock climbing this Saturday.

我冬天有時會去滑雪。

I sometimes go skiing in the winter.

腳踏車相關表達

• ride a bike：騎腳踏車
• get on / off a bike：上 / 下腳踏車
• cycling trail：（野外）腳踏車道
• bicycle lane：（市區）腳踏車專用道
• mountain bike：登山車
• cycling helmet：腳踏車安全帽
• lock：鎖
• handlebar：手把
• saddle：坐墊
• bike rack：腳踏車架

露營、水上活動、衝浪

露營

campsite, campground
露營場地、露營區

pitch a tent
搭帳篷

build a fire
生火

folding table / chair
折疊桌子 / 椅子

flashlight
手電筒

go camping 去露營
camping car, motorhome, camper, caravan 露營車
sleeping bag 睡袋
air mattress, air bed 充氣睡墊
camping stove 露營爐具
bug repellent 防蟲劑

SENTENCES TO USE

最近有很多地方都有露營區。	There are campsites in many places these days.
搭帳篷比我想像中難。	It is more difficult to pitch a tent than I thought.
我們打開摺疊桌椅然後吃飯。	We spread out our folding table and chairs and ate our meals.
為了和家人露營，他買了一輛露營車。	He bought a camping car to go camping with his family.
你用過充氣睡墊嗎？	Have you ever used an air mattress?
你去露營時一定要帶防蟲劑。	When you go camping, you have to take bug repellent.

swim[bathe] in the sea
在海裡游泳

 swimsuit
女性泳裝

 swimming trunk
男性泳褲

 sunbathing
日光浴

 deck chair
躺椅

 rubber ring
救生圈

 go surfing
衝浪

 windsurfing
風帆衝浪

 snorkeling
浮潛

 scuba-diving
水肺潛水

 **lifeguard**
救生員

sunscreen 防曬乳
jet ski 水上摩托車
wet suit 潛水衣
life preserver 救生圈、衣、背心等

SENTENCES TO USE

我很久沒來海邊游泳了。　It's been a long time since I went to swim in the sea.

很多人在尼斯海灘曬日光浴。　There were a lot of people sunbathing on the beaches in Nice.

我躺在躺椅上看書。　I read a book lying on the deck chair.

朱民常常去東海（日本海）衝浪。　Jumin often goes surfing to the East Sea.

救生員救了溺水的人。　The lifeguard saved the drowning man.

你去海邊時要擦好防曬。　You have to wear sunscreen thoroughly when you go to the beach.

CHAPTER

工作與經濟

———

Jobs & Economy

1 公司相關

company, firm 公司
large(big, major) company 大企業
conglomerate 企業集團
headquarters 本部、總部
branch 分部
subsidiary 子公司
affiliate 關係企業
subcontractor 外包商
chairperson, chairman 董事長
president 總裁
executive, director 主管、主任
department 部門

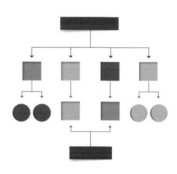

SENTENCES TO USE

很多年輕人想要在大公司工作。	Many young people want to get a job in large companies.
韓國的財團被稱作「chaebol（財閥）」。	The Korean conglomerate is called "chaebol."
亞馬遜公司總部在西亞圖。	Amazon's headquarters is in Seattle.
我哥哥在一間 P&T 外包商工作。	My brother works for a P&T subcontractor.
他在進入這家公司後，擔任主管超過20年。	He became an executive 20 years after joining the company.
我開始在行銷部門工作。	I started working in the marketing department.

board of directors 董事會
CEO 執行長 (**Chief Executive Officer**)
COO 營運長 (**Chief Operating Officer**)
CIO 資訊長 (**Chief Information Officer**)
CFO 財務長 (**Chief Financial Officer**)
CTO 技術長 (**Chief Technology Officer**)

employer 雇主
employee 受僱者
supervisor 主管、主任
assistant 助理
intern 實習生 (**internship** 實習)
secretary 祕書

SENTENCES TO USE

Google 的執行長桑德爾皮查伊是一位印度裔美國人。

Google's CEO is Indian American Sundar Pichai.

那家公司有超過100名員工。

The company has more than 100 employees.

我在一間廣告公司實習。

I worked as an intern at an advertising company.

職級
董事長、董事會主席：chairperson, chairman
副董事長：vice chairperson
執行長、總裁：CEO, president
副總裁：vice president
資深常務董事：senior managing director
常務董事：managing director
總經理：general manager, department head
副總經理：deputy general manager
組長：team manager
經理：manager, section chief
副理：assistant manager
一般職員、同事：associate

173

wage 薪水
payday 發薪日
pay rise 加薪
pay cut 減薪

special bonus
特別獎金

labor force
勞動力

employee welfare 員工福利
workday, working day 上班日
business day 營業日
working[office] hours 上班（營業）時間
labor union 工會
go on strike 罷工

SENTENCES TO USE

我們公司是每個月20日發薪。

我不認為我能夠期待今年加薪。

我們公司有很棒的員工福利。

今天不是上班日。

那家公司的上班時間是幾點到幾點？

工會決定罷工。

Our company's payday is the 20th of every month.

I don't think I can expect a pay rise this year.

Our company has good employee welfare.

Today is not a working day.

What's the working hours of that company?

The labor union decided to go on strike.

management
管理、經營

organization
組織

leadership
領導力

teamwork
團隊合作

interpersonal skills
社交技巧

project management
項目管理

time management
時間管理

decision making
下決策

problem solving
解決問題

data analysis
數據分析

negotiation
協商

customer service
顧客服務

SENTENCES TO USE

組織要成功，領導力和團隊合作很重要。　Leadership and teamwork are important for an organization to succeed.

社交技巧對於你的職場生活也很重要。　Interpersonal skills are also important in your work life.

應該要根據充分的資訊才能下決策。　Decision making should be based on sufficient information.

她從事客服工作。　She worked in customer service.

部門

management：管理、經營
PR (public relations)：公關
IT (information technology)：IT（信息和通訊技術）
production：生產
purchasing：採購

HR (human resources)：人事
R&D (research and development)：研發
accounts / finance：會計 / 財務
marketing：行銷
sales：銷售

各種職業

accountant 會計

actor / **actress** 演員

announcer 播報員、主持人

architect 建築師

artist 表演者、藝術家

astronaut 太空人

astronomer 天文學家

athlete 運動員

baby sitter 保母

bank clerk 銀行職員

banker 銀行家

barber 理髮師

book editor 書籍編輯

bus driver 公車司機

businessman / **businesswoman** 商人、企業家

butcher 肉舖老闆

carpenter 木工

cartoonist 漫畫家（**webtoonist** 網路漫畫家）

cashier 出納員

chef 廚師

civil officer 公務員

cleaner 清潔員

comedian 喜劇表演者

composer 作曲家

construction worker 建築工人

dentist 牙醫師

doctor 醫師

electrician 電機技師

engineer 工程師

farmer 農夫

fashion designer 時尚設計師

firefighter 消防員

flight attendant 空服員

hairdresser 美髮師

interior designer 室內設計師

interpreter 口譯員

janitor 警衛

journalist 記者

judge 法官

lawyer 律師

librarian 圖書館管理員

mechanic 維修技師

model 模特

movie director 電影導演

musician 音樂家

novelist 小說家

nurse 護理師

office worker 上班族

oriental medicine doctor 中醫師

painter 畫家

paramedic 急救護理人員

part-timer 兼職工

pharmacist 藥師

photographer 攝影師

physician 內科醫師

pilot 飛行員

plumber 水管工

police officer 警察

professor 教授

prosecutor 檢察官

psychiatrist 精神科醫師

psychologist 心理學家

receptionist 接待人員
reporter 報章記者
scientist 科學家
sculptor 雕刻家
security guard 保全
singer 歌手
storekeeper, shopkeeper 店主
surgeon 外科醫師
taxi driver 計程車司機
teacher 老師
tour guide 導遊
train driver 列車駕駛
translator 譯者
travel agent 旅行社代辦
TV director 電視劇導演、導播
TV writer 電視、綜藝編劇
vet, veterinarian 獸醫
waiter / **waitress** 服務生
writer 作家

UNIT 2 工作

go to work
上班

work from home
居家上班

get approval from
獲得 ～ 批准

make a weekly plan
建立每週計畫

finish work 結束工作
leave work[the office], **get off work** 下班
work full-time, be a full-time worker 全職工作
work part-time, be a part-time worker 兼職工作
temporary worker 非正規職、短期工作者
contract worker 約聘人員
work in shifts 輪班工作
be in charge of 負責 ～

SENTENCES TO USE

我希望我可以居家上班。	I wish I could work from home.
那件事需要取得組長同意。	It needs to get approval from our team manager.
你通常幾點下班？	What time do you usually get off work?
她是全職工作者。	She works full-time.
我是約聘人員。	I am a contract worker.
我希望由你來負責這個項目。	I want you to be in charge of this project.

have a meeting 開會
attend a meeting
出席會議

wrap up the meeting
結束會議

give a presentation
發表簡報

reach a consensus
取得共識

work overtime
加班

be promoted
被升遷
promotion 升遷

go on a business trip
出差

have a day off 休假一天
take a monthly holiday 休月假
take an annual vacation 休年假
call in sick 電話請病假
go on maternity / paternity leave 請產假
be on maternity / paternity leave 休產假中

SENTENCES TO USE

我們兩點有會議。	We'll have a meeting at two o'clock.
我下週要在總裁面前發表簡報。	I have to give a presentation in front of the president next week.
他被升為部門主管。	He was promoted to the department head.
我明天要去紐約出差。	I'm going on a business trip to New York tomorrow.
我休月假並去做健康檢查。	I took a monthly holiday and got a medical check-up.
我下個月要休產假。	I'm going on maternity leave next month.

就業

apply for a job 應徵職位
submit a résumé [CV (**curriculum vitae**)] 提交履歷
submit a letter of self-introduction 提交自我介紹信
have[do] a job interview 面試
get a job 求職
join[enter] a company 入職
post a job opening 發佈職缺 (**job opening** 職缺)
headhunt 獵頭
(**headhunter** 負責獵頭的人, **headhunting** 獵頭)
job seeker 求職者
job offer 工作機會、錄取通知
job opportunity 工作機會
qualifications 資格、條件

SENTENCES TO USE

我目前已經應徵了超過50份職缺。	I've applied for over 50 jobs so far.
請提交履歷和自我介紹信。	Please submit your résumé and a letter of self-introduction.
我明天要去公司面試。	I'm having a job interview with the company tomorrow.
如果本公司有職缺，我會再聯絡你。	I'll contact you if there's a job opening in our company.
每天都有很多求職者去就業博覽會。	Many job seekers come to the job fair every day.
那個職位的申請資格是什麼？	What are the qualifications for the job?

076

離職、失業

quit one's job 辭職
lose one's job 失業
get fired, be fired 被開除（**fire** 開除）
be laid off 被解僱（**lay somebody off** 解僱某人）
be unemployed[**jobless, out of work**] 失業中
unemployment 失業
unemployed[**jobless**] **person** 失業者

retire 退休（**retirement** 退休）
retired person 退休人員
receive one's pension 取得退休金、年金
receive severance pay 取得遣散費

SENTENCES TO USE

我因為健康因素辭職了。	I quit my job because I was in bad health.
他因為收賄被開除。	He was fired for taking bribes.
那家公司解僱百名以上員工。	The company laid off more than 100 workers.
她的丈夫已失業多年。	Her husband has been unemployed for several years.
你退休當時幾歲？	How old were you when you retired?
我預計65歲開始領取退休金。	I'm going to receive my pension from 65.

經濟相關

economy 經濟
industry 產業
enterprise, company, firm 企業、公司
corporation 企業、法人
demand 需求
supply 供給
production 生產
product 產品、商品
manufacture 製造、生產
manufacturer 製造者、生產者
goods 貨物、商品
service 服務、勞務

SENTENCES TO USE

世界經濟蕭條中。	The world economy is in recession.
他從事觀光業。	He's in the tourism industry.
價格根據供給和需求決定。	Prices are determined by supply and demand.
我負責開發新產品。	I work on developing new products.
聽說這個手機在韓國製造。	It says that this smartphone was manufactured in Korea.
那家公司是家具製造業者。	The company is a furniture manufacturer.

supplier 供應商
vendor 賣方
partner 合夥人
subcontractor 外包商
profit 利益、收益
loss 損失
have a gain[surplus], be in the black 有盈餘、順差
be in deficit, be in the red 有虧損、逆差
income 收益、所得
expense 支出、費用
revenue （政府的、組織的）收入、收益
cost (s) 費用、經費
expenditure 政府、組織、個人的支出

SENTENCES TO USE

供應商提供更低的價格。	The supplier offered a lower price.
他營運網路購物中心取得巨大收益。	He made a huge profit from running an Internet shopping mall.
貿易收支連年順差。	The trade balance has been in the black for years.
已實施各種為了低收入戶的福利政策。	Various welfare policies are carried out for low-income people.
你必須要平衡你的收益和支出。	You have to balance your income with your expenses.
那家公司如何縮減支出？	How can the company cut costs?

asset 資產
debt 債
liabilities 負債、債務
monopoly 獨佔、壟斷
investment 投資（**invest** 投資）
transaction 交易
economic downturn 景氣蕭條
economic recovery 景氣復甦
recession, depression 不景氣
economic boom 景氣繁榮
up-phase（景氣）繁榮期
inflation 通貨膨脹

SENTENCES TO USE

那家公司提供資產管理服務。

The company provides asset management services.

他因為賭博欠了很多債。

He is heavily in debt for gambling.

你把所有財產都拿去投資不動產嗎？

Did you invest all your property in real estate?

你認為經濟不景氣會持續嗎？

Do you think the economic downturn is going to last?

景氣繁榮時，生產、銷售、收益全都成長。

During the economic boom, productivity, sales and income all increase.

通貨膨脹是一段時間內的物價和服務費用都上漲。

Inflation is the increase in the prices of goods and services over a period of time.

inflation rate 物價上漲率
price index 物價指數
price stabilization 物價（價格）穩定
price fluctuation 物價（價格）浮動
capital 資本
labor 勞動
wholesale 批發
retail sale 零售
bankruptcy 破產
go bankrupt 破產

SENTENCES TO USE

這是最近房價變動的圖表。	This is a graph of the current state of housing price fluctuations.
想要成立公司需要多少資本？	How much capital do you need to set up a company?
他營運的建設公司破產了。	The construction company he was running went bankrupt.

各種產業

advertising 廣告　　　　　agriculture, farming 農業
construction 建設　　　　　education 教育
electronics 電子技術　　　　entertainment 演藝
fashion 時尚　　　　　　　finance 金融
fishing 漁業　　　　　　　forestry 林業
healthcare 醫療　　　　　　journalism 新聞業
livestock farming 畜牧業　　manufacturing 製造業
mining 礦業　　　　　　　pharmaceutical 製藥
real estate 不動產　　　　　shipping 物流
tourism 觀光　　　　　　　transportation 運輸

金融、股市、稅金

金融

finance
金融、財務、財政

currency
貨幣

cash
現金
（**coin** 硬幣, **bill** 紙鈔）

check
支票

credit card 信用卡
debit card 簽帳卡

ATM
（**automatic teller
machine**）自動提款機

**PIN
number**
個人密碼

**mobile
banking**
行動銀行

bankbook 存摺
bank account number 銀行帳戶
online banking 網路銀行

SENTENCES TO USE

哪個部門管理國家財政？	Which department manages the national finances?
大部分歐洲國家使用單一貨幣——歐元。	Most European countries use a single currency, the euro.
信用卡和簽帳卡有何不同？	How are credit cards and debit cards different?
地鐵站有自動提款機嗎？	Is there an ATM at the subway station?
最近人們常用行動銀行。	People use mobile banking a lot these days.
請告訴我你的銀行帳戶。	Please let me know your bank account number.

interest 利息
interest rate 利率
open / **close a bank account** 開設 / 關閉銀行帳戶
save money 儲蓄
get into debt 貸款
deposit money 存款
withdraw money 提款
remit, send[transfer] money 匯款
put ~ into a fixed deposit account 存入定期存款帳戶
put[pay] ~ into an installment savings account 存入零存整付儲蓄帳戶
get a bank loan, get a loan from the bank 向銀行貸款
take out / **pay off a mortgage** 取得 / 償還抵押貸款

SENTENCES TO USE

最近存款利率只有2%。	These days, the interest rate on deposits is only about 2 percent.
關閉你再也不會用的銀行帳戶。	Close the bank account that you don't use any more.
請匯款給他。	Please remit the expenses to him.
當我得到一大筆錢,我就會存到定存帳戶。	When I get a large sum of money, I put it into a fixed deposit account.
跟銀行貸款越來越難。	It's getting harder and harder to get a loan from a bank.

股票

stock exchange
證券（股票）交易所

buy stocks
買股票

sell stocks
賣股票

make / lose money in stocks
在股市中賺錢／賠錢

税金

pay tax
繳稅

get[receive] a tax refund
收到退稅

tax cut
減稅

tax hike
增稅

deduction of tax
扣除稅額

SENTENCES TO USE

韓國證券交易所在哪裡？	Where is the Korea Stock Exchange?
你買過股票嗎？	Have you ever bought stocks?
我的叔叔在股票中賠了很多錢。	My uncle lost a lot of money in stocks.
有很多人沒有繳稅。	There are a lot of people who don't pay taxes.
我要如何取得退稅？	How do I get my tax refund?
減稅可以促進消費。	Tax cuts can help boost consumer sentiment.

Many job seekers come to the job fair every day.

JOB

I've applied for over 50 jobs so far.

CHAPTER
10

購物

Shopping

各種商店

market
市場

traditional market 傳統市場
local market 地方市場

street market
街市、集市

department store
百貨公司

shopping mall
購物中心

supermarket
超市

convenience store
便利商店

flea market 跳蚤市場
grocery (**store**) 雜貨店、超市

SENTENCES TO USE

地方政府試著活化地方市場。	Local governments are trying to boost local markets.
逛一下街市很有趣。	It was fun to look around the street market.
附近有百貨公司或購物中心嗎？	Is there a department store or a shopping mall nearby?
最近在便利商店什麼都有。	There's everything in convenience stores these days.
我在跳蚤市場買了一些好東西。	I bought some nice things at the flea market.
去雜貨店買一些醋和黃瓜。	Go to the grocery store and get some vinegar and cucumbers.

**baker's,
bakery**
麵包店

**butcher shop,
the butcher's**
肉鋪

fish dealer
魚販、魚行

**fruit
shop[store]**
水果攤、水果行

rice store[shop]
米舖

furniture store
家具店

**electronics store,
electrical appliances store**
電器用品店、家電用品店

**clothing
shop[store]**
衣飾店

**lingerie shop[store],
underwear shop[store]**
內衣店

shoe shop[store]
鞋店

**jewelry
store**
珠寶店

SENTENCES TO USE

當我走過麵包店時，味道好香。   It smells good when I walk past the bakery.

我在肉鋪買了600克的豬肉。   I bought 600 grams of pork at the butcher's.

那條街有很多家具店。   There are many furniture stores on the street.

我需要買台新電視，
所以要去家電用品店。   I need to buy a new TV so I'm going to the electronics store.

我在內衣店買了一些內褲和襪子。   I bought some panties and socks at the underwear store.

以前這裡有家珠寶店。   There used to be a jewelry store here.

bookstore
書店

stationery shop[store]
文具店

flower[florist] shop
花店

hardware store
五金行

pharmacy, chemist's
藥局

drugstore
藥妝店

barber shop 理髮廳
beauty salon, beauty parlor, hair salon 美容院、髮廊
real estate agency 不動產仲介營業處
laundry, dry cleaner's 洗衣店

SENTENCES TO USE

很可惜最近沒有地方書店。	I'm sorry there is no local bookstore these days.
我的姪女喜歡去文具店。	My niece likes to go to the stationery shop.
五金行有賣拖把嗎？	Do they sell mops in the hardware store?
附近有週日營業的藥局嗎？	Is there a pharmacy in this neighborhood that opens on Sunday?
我今天要去美容院剪頭髮。	I'm going to the beauty parlor to get my hair cut today.
附近有很多不動產仲介營業處。	There are a lot of real estate agencies around here.

百貨公司的店家

cosmetics 化妝品
men's wear 男裝
women's wear 女裝
children's wear 童裝
lingerie 內衣
sportswear 運動服
bags 包
shoes 鞋
toys 玩具
stationery 文具
electrical appliances, home appliances 家電用品
home furnishings 家具和配件
kitchenware 廚房用品
food court 美食街
duty-free shop 免稅店
customer service center 顧客服務中心

購物相關

window-shop, do window shopping 櫥窗購物
shop around 四處逛
be out of stock 無庫存
bargain[**haggle**] **(over)** 殺價
give a discount 給予折扣
pay in installments 分期付款
exchange A for B 把 A 換成 B
get a refund (**on**) 取得退款

try on
試穿

be on sale
販售中、特價中

pay in cash
用現金付款

pay by credit card
用信用卡付款

SENTENCES TO USE

我四處逛以貨比三家。	I shopped around for bargains.
M尺寸無庫存。	M size is out of stock.
我的媽媽會在市場買東西時殺價。	My mother bargains when she buys things in the market.
我想要退款。	I'd like to get a refund on this.
我可以試穿嗎？	Can I try this on?
你想要付現金還是信用卡？	Would you like to pay in cash or by credit card?

operating〔business〕hours 營業時間
fixed price 定價
special offer 特價、特價品
shelves 展示櫃、陳列架
fitting room 試衣間
receipt 收據

price tag
標價

promote 宣傳
promotion
宣傳、促銷

shopping cart
購物車

basket
購物籃

shopping bag
購物袋

clerk 店員
cashier
收銀員

cash register
收銀機

customer
顧客

checkout〔counter〕
結帳台

SENTENCES TO USE

那家百貨公司的營業時間是幾點到幾點？ What's the business hours of the department store?

我們這裡定價販售。 We sell them here at the fixed price.

請問試衣間在哪裡？ Where is the fitting room?

沒有購物車。 There's no shopping cart.

我隨身攜帶購物袋。 I carry my shopping bag with me.

結帳台在哪邊？ Which way is the checkout counter?

網路購物、海外直購

網路購物

Internet shopping mall 網路購物中心
create an account 建立帳號（**account** 帳號）
membership 會員資格（身份）

join a shopping mall 加入網路購物中心
log in to, sign in to 登入
log out of, sign out of 登出

category 商品類別
add to cart[bag] 放入購物車
add to wish list 放入願望清單
edit cart 修改購物車

order 訂購
enter shipping address 輸入配送地點
shipping information 配送資訊（收件人、地址、電話、姓名等等）
payment information 付款資訊（付款方式、信用卡種類等等）
continue to payment, proceed to checkout 付款進行中

order number 訂單編號
tracking number 訂單追蹤編號
shipping and handling charge, delivery charge 運費
charge ~ for shipping (and handling) 收取運費
send ~ by C. O. D. (cash[collect] on delivery) 貨到付款
deliver ~ for free 免運費
free shipping 免運費
return item 退貨
choose items to return 選擇要退貨的物品

overseas purchase 海外直購
foreign site 海外網站
order from abroad 從海外直購（非代購）
Black Friday 黑色星期五（11月最後一個星期五，商家會有大幅折扣優惠）
Cyber Monday 網路星期一（黑色星期五後的星期一，商家會有大幅折扣優惠）
Boxing Day 節禮日（聖誕節隔天，商家會有折扣優惠）
shipping address 收件地址
billing address 帳單地址（信用卡發卡地址）
PCCC (Personal Customs Clearance Code),
PCC (Personal Clearance Code), Customs ID Number 個人清關認證碼
sales tax 海外購物附加消費稅
back order 無庫存時下訂（到貨時再配送）
off load 因為飛機問題，訂購的物品會延後空運
return label 退貨單（退貨時務必印出貼於箱子外）

CHAPTER

11

國家

──

Nation

政治

politics 政治、政治觀點
politician 政治人物（常指參政者）
statesman 政治家（常指經驗豐富的領導者）
political power 政權（政治權力）

government 政府、政體、統治
administration 行政、行政部門

legislation 立法
legislature 立法機關
legislator, lawmaker 立法者、立法委員

SENTENCES TO USE

因為政治與我們的生活息息相關，所以我們必須關注。

Politics is closely related to our lives, so we should pay attention to it.

我朋友的爸爸曾是知名政治人物。

My friend's father was a famous politician.

取得政權是政黨的目標。

The goal of a political party is to take political power.

政府正在努力穩定不動產的價格。

The government is trying to stabilize real estate prices.

國會的工作是立法，也就是制定法律。

What the National Assembly does is legislation, that is to enact laws.

National Assembly 國會
member of the National Assembly 國會議員

jurisdiction 司法權
judiciary 司法機關

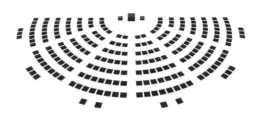

political party 政黨
ruling party 執政黨
opposition party 在野黨
progressive 進步派的、進步主義的
conservative 保守派的、保守主義的
liberal 自由主義的

SENTENCES TO USE

國家將權力分給行政、立法、司法三個機關。
The state power is divided into the administration, the legislature and the judiciary.

執政黨是取得政權的政黨。
The ruling party is the party that holds the power.

在野黨當然要批判並牽制政府。
The opposition party should criticize and check the government.

他的傾向是進步派還是保守派？
Is he progressive or conservative?

democracy 民主主義
democratic 民主主義的、民主的

republic
共和國

dictatorship
獨裁（國家）

monarchy
君主制

anarchy
無政府

parliamentary democracy 議會制民主
totalitarianism 極權主義（**totalitarian** 極權主義者、極權主義的）
socialism 社會主義（**socialist** 社會主義者、社會主義的）
capitalism 資本主義（**capitalist** 資本主義者、資本主義的）
communism 共產主義（**communist** 共產主義者、共產主義的）

SENTENCES TO USE

民主主義的相反是社會主義還是共產主義？	Is the opposition of democracy socialism or communism?
共和國是主權在民的國家。	A republic is a country where sovereignty resides with its people.
極權主義體制中，個人是為了集團而存在。	In a totalitarian regime, individuals exist only for groups.
資本主義不是政治體制，是經濟體制。	Capitalism is not a political system but an economic system.
建立有效的教育政策是必要的。	It is necessary to establish an effective education policy.
那位國會議員今年提出最多法案。	The lawmaker proposed the most bills this year.
總理和各部會首長由總統任命。	The Prime Minister and the Ministers are appointed by the President.

establish a policy 建立政策
propose a bill 提出法案
pass a bill 通過法案
appoint 任命
impeach 彈劾（**impeachment** 彈劾）

president 總統
vice president 副總統
prime minister 首相、總理
minister 部長
vice minister 次長

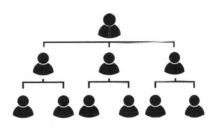

政府機構

財政部	Ministry of Economy and Finance
教育部	Ministry of Education
外交部	Ministry of Foreign Affairs
法務部	Ministry of Justice
國防部	Ministry of National Defense
衛生福利部	Ministry of Health and Welfare
勞動部	Ministry of Employment and Labor

vote 投票、投票表決
voter 投票者、投票權人
voting right, right to vote 投票權
hold a referendum on 實施公民投票
elect 選舉
have|hold| an election 實施選舉（**election** 選舉）
election day 選舉投票日
presidential election 總統選舉
parliamentary election, National Assembly election 國會議員選舉

SENTENCES TO USE

我今天早上很早就去投票。	I voted early this morning.
韓國人民滿18歲擁有投票權。	Koreans have the right to vote at the age of 18.
英國舉行脫歐公投。	The United Kingdom held a referendum on Brexit.
地方政府首長由人民選出。	The heads of local governments are elected by the people.

run for the National Assembly
參選國會議員

run for presidency 參選總統
run for mayor 參選市長
candidate 候選人

go on a campaign, canvass
進行競選活動、遊說

support a candidate 支持候選人
election campaign 競選活動

poll, opinion poll, opinion survey, public opinion poll
輿論調查

conduct a (public opinion) poll
進行輿論調查

election result
選舉結果

win / lose an election
勝選 / 敗選

SENTENCES TO USE

那位前主播參選過國會議員。	The former anchor ran for the National Assembly.
那位候選人的家族正在進行競選活動。	The candidate's family is going on a campaign.
你有支持的候選人嗎？	Do you have a candidate to support?
根據最新的輿論調查結果，執政黨支持率微幅上升。	According to a recent poll, the ruling party's approval rating has risen slightly.
什麼時候會發表選舉結果？	When will the election result be announced?
那位現任議員敗選了嗎？	Did the incumbent lose the election?

3 外交

diplomacy 外交
diplomat 外交官
foreign policy 外交政策
Ministry of
Foreign Affairs 外交部

ally, allied nations 同盟國
make an alliance 結盟

embassy 大使館
ambassador 大使

negotiate 協商、交涉（**negotiation** 協商、交涉）
intervene 仲裁、干預（**intervention** 協調、仲裁、干預）

SENTENCES TO USE

外交就是不同國家間在政治上、經濟上、文化上建立關係。	Diplomacy is the establishment of political, economic and cultural relations with other countries.
我小時候的願望是成為外交官。	My childhood dream was to be a diplomat.
日本不是韓國的盟國。	Japan is not an ally of Korea.
那個國家有韓國大使館嗎？	Is there a Korean Embassy in that country?
北韓和美國正在協商無核化。	North Korea and the U.S. are negotiating denuclearization.
美國很難直接干涉香港現況。	It is difficult for the United States to intervene directly in the Hong Kong situation.

sign[form, conclude] a treaty
締約

sign[conclude] an agreement
簽訂協議

have a summit 舉行高峰會
inter-Korean summit 南北韓高峰會

international organization
國際機構

---

declare 宣布（**declaration** 宣言、宣布）
impose[call for] a sanction 實施制裁
protocol 外交禮儀、國際公約
friction 矛盾、衝突
refugee 難民

SENTENCES TO USE

為了結束鴉片戰爭，英國和清朝於1842年簽訂南京條約。

To end the Opium War, the United Kingdom and Qing Dynasty signed the Nanjing Treaty in 1842.

韓國和美國在2007年簽訂自由貿易協定。

South Korea and the United States signed a free trade agreement (FTA) in 2007.

南北韓高峰會談於2018年的4月27日在板門店舉行。

The inter-Korean summit was held at Panmunjom on April 27, 2018.

美國、英國和中國的領導人以〈波茨坦宣言〉促令日本投降。

Through the Potsdam Declaration, the heads of the United States, Britain and China recommended Japan surrender.

美國正對北韓實施經濟制裁。

The United States is imposing economic sanctions on North Korea.

在2018年，有超過500名葉門難民進入濟州島。

In 2018, more than 500 Yemeni refugees entered Jeju Island.

4 軍事

military 軍、軍隊、軍的、軍事的　　**military power, military force** 軍事力量
military action 軍事行動、軍事作戰　　**armed forces**（國家的）軍隊
join the army 加入軍隊、入伍　　**do one's military service** 服役
be discharged from the military service 退伍

soldier
軍人、士兵

officer
軍官

army
軍、軍隊、陸軍 (the~)

navy
海軍

air force
空軍

the Marines,
the Marine Corps
海軍陸戰隊

SENTENCES TO USE

截至2019年，韓國軍事力量世界排名第七。
As of 2019, South Korea's military power is the seventh-largest in the world.

大部分的國家都擁有軍隊。
Most countries have armed forces.

我的爸爸曾在前線服役。
My father did his military service in the front line.

你的弟弟什麼時候退伍？
When will your brother be discharged from the military service?

韓國空軍的象徵是Boramae，也就是獵鷹。
The symbol of the Korean Air Force is Boramae, or tamed hawk.

那位歌手自願加入海軍陸戰隊。
The singer volunteered for the Marine Corps.

attack 攻擊
defend 防禦
defense 防禦

battle 戰鬥
enemy troops[forces] 敵軍
allied forces 聯軍

terrorist 恐怖主義者
terrorist attack 恐怖攻擊

weapons of mass destruction
大規模殺傷性武器
disarmament
裁減軍備

develop nuclear weapons 發展核武
denuclearize 無核化
denuclearization 無核化
denuclearization talks / **agreement** 無核化會談 / 協議
denuclearization of the Korean peninsula 韓半島無核化

SENTENCES TO USE

美國和英國於2003年攻擊伊拉克。

The United States and Britain attacked Iraq in 2003.

鳴梁海戰中，朝鮮水軍成功抵抗日本。

In the Battle of Myeongnyang, the navy of Joseon won a victory over Japan.

同盟國的軍隊在第二次世界大戰中贏得勝利。

In World War II, the Allied Forces won.

2001年的恐怖攻擊造成世界貿易中心兩棟大樓倒塌。

Two World Trade Center buildings collapsed in 2001 due to a terrorist attack.

北韓從1960年代開始發展核武。

North Korea has been developing nuclear weapons since the 1960s.

韓國總統努力讓韓半島無核化。

The Korean President is working to denuclearize the Korean Peninsula.

12

社會

Society

懷孕、生產、育兒

懷孕、生產

be pregnant 懷孕
pregnancy 懷孕
pregnant woman
孕婦

do[take] a pregnancy test
驗孕
pregnancy test kit
驗孕棒

have morning sickness
孕吐

give birth to a baby,
deliver a baby
生小孩、分娩
childbirth 生產、分娩

newborn baby
新生兒

umbilical cord
臍帶

SENTENCES TO USE

請讓位給孕婦。	Please give your seat to the pregnant woman.
盡快去驗孕。	Do a pregnancy test as soon as possible.
我有嚴重孕吐。	I had bad morning sickness.
那位爸爸剪掉新生兒的臍帶。	The father cut the umbilical cord of the newborn baby.
我自然產生下老大。	I delivered my oldest child by natural birth.
我的姊姊是剖腹產生下的。	My sister was born by Caesarean section.

deliver(give birth to) ~ by natural birth 自然產
be born by natural birth 自然產出生
have a Caesarean section 剖腹產
be born by Caesarean section 剖腹產出生
miscarry, have a miscarriage 流產
birth rate 出生率
promote(encourage) childbirth 鼓勵生育
pay a childbirth grant 給付生育獎勵
impose birth control 實施節育

SENTENCES TO USE

截至2018年，韓國的出生率是每位女性0.977個孩子，全世界最低。	As of 2018, Korea's birth rate was 0.977 births per fertile woman, the lowest in the world.
政府用多種方式來鼓勵生育。	The government is encouraging childbirth in a variety of ways.
政府在過去實施節育。	In the past, the government imposed birth control.

剖腹產

剖腹產的英文是 Caesarean section。Caesarean 是 Caesar（古羅馬的政治家凱薩）的形容詞型態。Caesarean section 的德文是 Kaiserschnitt，日文漢字直譯為「帝王切開」。

傳說凱薩是用此方法出生，因此 Caesarean section 是源自於他的名字，此和事實並不符。古羅馬作家老普林尼利用含有「切開」之意的 caesum 創造了 sectio caesarea 一詞，因為 caesarea 的發音和凱薩相似，所以產生了誤會。無論如何，後者聽起來更真實吧？

get an abortion 墮胎、終止妊娠（**abortion** 墮胎、終止妊娠）
support abortion 贊成墮胎（**pro-choice** 贊成墮胎的）
oppose abortion 反對墮胎（**pro-life** 反對墮胎的）

postpartum care 產後照護
postpartum care center 月子中心
recover after childbirth,
get[receive] postpartum care 產後護理、坐月子
be on maternity leave 休產假中（**maternity leave** 產假）
be on childcare leave 休育嬰假中（**childcare leave** 育嬰假）

SENTENCES TO USE

墮胎在我國違法。	Abortion is illegal in our country.
天主教反對墮胎。	The Catholic Church opposes abortion.
你贊成墮胎還是反對？	Are you pro-choice or pro-life?
現今有許多媽媽在月子中心接受產後照護。	Nowadays, most mothers get postpartum care in postpartum care centers.
她正在休產假。	She is on maternity leave now.
你的育嬰假可以休幾天？	How long can you use your childcare leave?

091

育兒

bring up(raise) a baby
養育小孩

breastfeed 餵母乳
breastfeeding 餵母乳

bottle feed 瓶餵
bottle feeding 瓶餵
baby bottle 奶瓶

change a diaper
換尿布

stroller
嬰兒車

potty
嬰幼兒尿盆

baby food
嬰幼兒食品

childcare facilities
托兒設施

daycare center
托育中心

nanny, baby sitter
保母

SENTENCES TO USE

餵母乳對媽媽和小孩都有好處。	Breastfeeding is good for both mothers and children.
奶瓶用熱水消毒好嗎？	Would it be good to disinfect the baby bottle with hot water?
你換過尿布嗎？	Have you ever changed a diaper?
我的小孩現在還是想坐嬰兒車。	My child still wants to ride in a stroller.
我自己做嬰幼兒食品。	I make my own baby food.
小孩幾歲可以去托育中心？	At what age can a child go to a daycare center?

2 人權、性別平等、社會福利

protect[support] human rights 保障（擁護）人權
violate[infringe on] human rights 侵害（踐踏）人權
welfare policy 福利政策
social worker 社工

gender equality
性別平等

gender discrimination
性別歧視

Me Too movement
Me Too 運動

welfare 福利 / **public welfare** 公共福利
/ **social welfare** 社工

SENTENCES TO USE

現在的搜查方式正在侵害人權。	The current investigation method is infringing on human rights.
對於性別平等的理解改善了很多。	The perception of gender equality has improved a lot.
Me Too 運動始於2017年的好萊塢。	The Me Too movement started in Hollywood in 2017.
政府實施許多公共福利政策。	The government is implementing various public welfare policies.
韓國正從高齡化社會步入高齡社會。	Korea is moving from an aging society to an aged society.

welfare for senior citizens[the elderly] 老人福利
aging society 高齡化社會
aged society 高齡社會
basic old-age pension 老年基本保證年金
old-age pensioner 老年年金領取者

child benefit
兒童津貼

**support a
single-parent family**
補助單親家庭

**welfare for
the disabled
[handicapped]**
身障者福利

give aid to[relieve] the poor 救濟貧民
national basic livelihood security recipient 基本生活保障對象
increase welfare budget 增加社會福利預算
universal welfare 普及式社會福利
selective welfare 選擇式社會福利

高齡化社會、高齡社會、超高齡社會
- aging society（高齡化社會）：總人口中65歲以上的人口佔7%以上
- aged society（高齡社會）：14%以上
- super-aged society（超高齡社會）：20%以上

普及式社會福利、選擇式社會福利
- universal welfare（普及式社會福利）：提供給全國人民。包括健康保險、國民年金、學校免費供餐、老年基本保證年金、兒童津貼、托育津貼、育兒津貼等等。
- selective welfare（選擇式社會福利）：只提供給需要的人。包括國民基本生活保障、補助單親家庭、身障者福利等等。

3 災害、事故

災害

natural disaster 自然災害　　　　**human disaster** 人為災害

fire
火災

forest fire
山火、森林火災

earthquake 地震
aftershock 餘震

heavy rainfall
豪雨

**localized
heavy rain**
局部豪雨

typhoon
颱風

heavy snowfall
暴雪

flood
洪水

drought
乾旱

landslide
土石流

tsunami
海嘯

SENTENCES TO USE

即使無法防止自然災害，也要預防人為災害。

Even if natural disasters cannot be prevented, human disasters should be prevented.

在加州，幾乎每年都會發生很大的森林火災。

A big forest fire occurs almost every year in California.

韓國再也無法免於地震。

Korea is no longer free from earthquakes.

局部豪雨會導致土石流。

Localized heavy rain can cause landslides.

今年10月有颱風來。

There is a typhoon coming in October this year.

當年的春夏曾經發生嚴重乾旱。

There was a severe drought from spring to summer that year.

heat wave 酷暑
shelter, refuge 避難處、收容所

cold wave 寒流
refugee 難民

事故

have a car(traffic) accident
發生車禍

have a car crash
發生相撞車禍
have a fender bender 發生輕微車禍

air crash, (air) plane crash
飛機失事

suffer shipwreck
發生船難

survive an accident / a crash / a shipwreck
從事故／車禍、空難／船難中倖存

call an ambulance
打給救護車

go to an ER
送往急診室
be taken to an ER
被送往急診室

SENTENCES TO USE

今天首爾發布寒流警報。	A cold wave warning was issued in Seoul today.
地震難民正待在避難處。	Refugees from the earthquake are staying in the shelter.
我今天回家的路上發生小車禍。	I had a fender bender on my way home today.
那位歌手於空難中身亡。	The singer died in an airplane crash.
那些船難倖存者遭遇很大的心理創傷。	Those who survived the shipwreck suffered great trauma.
請幫我叫救護車！	Call an ambulance, please!

commit a crime 犯罪
violent crime 重大犯罪（殺人、綁架、搶劫、性暴力等等）
suspect 嫌疑犯
get ~ stolen, be robbed of ~ 被偷竊、被搶劫

cyber crime
網路犯罪

criminal **victim**
犯人　被害者

theft, burglary
竊盜

robbery
搶劫

**have one's pocket picked,
be(get) pick pocketed**
遇到扒手
pickpocket 扒手

con, swindle
詐騙
fraud
詐騙、詐騙人員

speeding
超速
speeding ticket
超速罰單

SENTENCES TO USE

你活著就不該犯罪。	You must live without committing a crime.
警察將嫌疑犯放到通緝名單中。	The police put the suspect on the wanted list.
他的平板電腦被偷了。	He got his tablet PC stolen.
我在羅馬遇到扒手。	I had my pocket picked in Rome.
你被詐騙過嗎？	Have you ever been swindled?
我被開了一張超速罰單。	I got a speeding ticket.

**be[get]
hacked into**
被駭

murder 殺人
murderer 殺人犯
serial murder 連續殺人
serial killer 連續殺人犯

**assault,
violence**
暴行、暴力

arson 縱火
arsonist 縱火犯
**set ~ on fire,
set fire to**
在 ～ 縱火

kidnap
綁架
kidnapper
綁架犯

**sexual
violence**
性暴力
（性騷擾、性侵害）

**sexual
harassment**
性騷擾

**sexual
assault**
性侵害、性暴力

rape 強暴
（**rapist** 強暴犯）

**white-collar
crime**
白領犯罪

SENTENCES TO USE

我的 Instagram 帳號被駭。

I got hacked into my Instagram account.

那名連續殺人犯在20多年後被逮。

The serial killer was captured after more than 20 years.

他被指控施予暴行。

He was charged with assault.

2008年，一名老人在崇禮門縱火。

An old man set Sungnyemun on fire in 2008.

有一些專門負責性暴力的律師。

There are lawyers who specialize in sexual violence.

白領犯罪是由那些擁有社會權勢、經濟或技術優勢者所犯下的罪行。

White-collar crime is committed by those who have social, economic, or technological power.

bribe 賄賂、賄賂某人
bribery 賄賂

embezzle
侵佔、貪污

take drugs
吸毒

drug dealing
毒品交易

police officer
警察

patrol car
警車

evidence 證據
clue 線索

fingerprint
指紋

investigate 搜查
police station 警察局 / **police box** 派出所
prosecutor 檢察官 / **the prosecution** 檢方、控方律師
scientific investigation 科學搜查

SENTENCES TO USE

那名校長因為賄賂被撤職。 The principal of the school was dismissed for bribery charges.

檢察官們在沒有明確證據下起訴案件。 The prosecutors indicted the case without any apparent evidence.

他們多虧指紋才能夠抓到犯人。 They were able to catch the criminal thanks to the fingerprint.

警察正在搜查案件。 The police are investigating the case.

我家附近有一間派出所。 There's a police box right near my house.

科學搜查技術持續發展。 Scientific investigation technology continues to develop.

chase
追逐

flee
逃跑

arrest
逮補

handcuffs
手銬

interrogate 詢問、訊問
interrogation 詢問、訊問
confess 自白

be taken into custody
被拘留

witness 目擊者
request / issue a warrant 申請令狀 / 發布令狀
arrest warrant 拘捕令
search warrant 搜索票
cold case 未結案件

SENTENCES TO USE

一名男子在犯罪現場被逮補。	A man was arrested at the scene of the crime.
檢察官表示該嫌疑犯已自白。	The prosecutor said that the suspect had confessed.
這名男性最後被拘留。	The man was eventually taken into custody.
我以目擊者身份去警察局。	I went to the police station as a witness to the case.
法院發布令狀。	The court issued a warrant.
有正努力解決未結案件的警察。	There are police officers who are trying to solve the cold cases.

observe[keep, obey, abide by] the law 遵守法律
apply the law 施行法律
court 法庭
try 審判 / **trial** 審判
case 案件
file a suit[lawsuit] 提起訴訟（**lawsuit** 訴訟）
accuse 控告、告發
indict 起訴
lawyer 律師
prosecutor 檢察官

SENTENCES TO USE

大部分的人都會遵守法律。	Most people abide by the law.
法律應該適用於每一個人。	The law should be applied equally to everyone.
該男子因殺人受審。	The man was tried for murder.
她對她先生提起訴訟。	She filed a lawsuit against her husband.
一個市民團體告發該政治人物。	A civic group accused the politician.
請一位律師需要花費很多錢嗎？	Does it cost us a lot of money to hire a lawyer?

judge
法官、審判

**defendant,
the accused**
被告

plaintiff
原告

juror
陪審員

jury
陪審團

rule
裁定

ruling, decision
裁定

---

witness（法庭上的）證人
give testimony（在法庭上）證言
plead, defend 申辯
dismiss 駁回

SENTENCES TO USE

該法官警告檢察官。	The judge warned the prosecutor.
該被告沒有出庭。	The defendant did not appear in court.
刑事案件的原告是檢察官。	The plaintiff in a criminal case is the prosecutor.
韓國於2008年開始實施陪審團制度。	The jury system has been implemented in Korea since 2008.
法官已裁定。	The judge ruled.
他出庭並提供證言。	He attended the trial and gave testimony.

sentence 宣判、判決
be sentenced to 被判刑 ～
final trial 終審
be found guilty 被判有罪
be found not guilty 被判無罪
fine, impose a fine 處以罰金、罰鍰（**fine** 罰金、罰鍰）
appeal 上訴
serve ~ in prison 入獄服刑
go to jail[prison], be sent to[put into] jail[prison] 入獄

SENTENCES TO USE

法庭對被告判處無期徒刑。	The court sentenced the defendant to life imprisonment.
該連續殺人犯被判以死刑。	The serial killer was sentenced to death.
該男子在審判中被判有罪。	The man was found guilty at the trial.
那位檢察官立刻提起上訴。	The prosecutor appealed immediately.
他在監獄服刑了17年。	He served 17 years in prison.

法院的種類
Supreme Court 最高法院
High Court 高等法院
District[Local] Court 地方法院
Family Court 家事法庭

審判
一審：the first trial
二審（上訴審）：the second trial
三審（終審）：the third trial, the final trial

Even if natural
disasters
cannot be
prevented,
HUMAN
DISASTERS
SHOULD BE
PREVENTED.

6 媒體、輿論

the media 媒體（**the mass media** 大眾媒體）
journalism 新聞業
news agency 新聞通訊社
article 報導
editorial 社論
cover 取材報導
correspondent 特派記者
breaking news 突發新聞、最新消息

the press
記者、新聞界

**morning / evening
(news) paper**
早報 / 晚報

**online
newspaper**
網路新聞

**journalist,
reporter**
記者

SENTENCES TO USE

通訊社提供新聞給報紙和廣播電視媒體。	The news agency provides news to newspapers and broadcasters.
他的爸爸曾是駐中國的特派記者。	Her father was a correspondent in China.
電視會以最新消息播報審判結果。	The results of the trial are coming out in breaking news on TV.
我們需要思考媒體的角色和責任。	We need to think about the role and responsibility of the press.
現今有許多人在網路上閱讀新聞文章。	Nowadays, most people read newspaper articles on the Internet.
記者多年來一直在取材報導該案件。	The journalist has been covering the case for years.

have an interview（記者）採訪
give an interview（採訪對象）接受採訪
interviewer 採訪者
interviewee 受訪者

broadcast 播送
broadcaster, broadcasting station
[**company**] 廣播電臺、電視臺（公司）
TV / **radio station** 電視臺 / 廣播電臺
Internet broadcast 網路播送
live broadcast 直播

give[**hold**] **a press conference** 開記者會（**press conference** 記者會）
weekly / **monthly magazine** 週刊 / 月刊
personal broadcasting 個人播送、個人廣播
one-person media 一人媒體

SENTENCES TO USE

我昨天接受一家電視臺採訪。	I gave an interview to a TV station yesterday.
他們的演唱會經由電視播放。	Their concert was broadcast on TV.
我的姊姊在一家電臺當廣播製作人。	My sister works as a radio producer at a broadcasting station.
那位歌手開了個引退記者會。	The singer gave a press conference about his retirement.
最近有許多人在做個人廣播。	There are a lot of people doing personal broadcasting these days.
一人媒體有其優缺點。	One-person media has light and shadow.

believe in 信仰～（宗教）
convert to 改信～

Christianity 基督教
Christian 基督教徒
Catholic Church
天主堂
Catholic 天主教徒
Catholicism 天主教
Protestantism 新教
Protestant 新教徒

Buddhism 佛教
Buddhist 佛教徒

Won Buddhism
韓國圓佛教

Won Buddhist
韓國圓佛教徒

Islam
伊斯蘭教

Muslim
伊斯蘭教徒

Hinduism 印度教
Hindu 印度教徒

Judaism 猶太教
Judaist, Jew 猶太教徒

* **shamanism** 巫覡宗教
* **Confucianism** 儒教
* **Taoism** 道教

SENTENCES TO USE

他婚後改信天主教。

He converted to Catholicism after he got married.

天主教和新教都屬於基督教。

Both the Catholic Church and the Protestantism belong to Christianity.

韓國圓佛教創於1910年代的韓國。

Won Buddhism originated in Korea in the 1910s.

穆斯林不吃豬肉。

Muslims do not eat pork.

猶太教不承認新約聖經。

Judaism does not recognize the New Testament.

巫覡宗教在過去被廣泛傳播。

In the past, shamanism was widespread.

099

Bible
聖經

* **Buddhist scriptures**
佛教經典

go to mass
（去教堂）望彌撒

attend a service
做禮拜

be baptized
受洗
baptism 洗禮

attend / hold a Buddhist service
參加法會／辦法會

cathedral
大教堂（有主教的教堂）

Catholic Church
教堂

church
教會

Buddhist temple
寺廟、佛教廟宇

mosque
清真寺

synagogue
猶太會堂

SENTENCES TO USE

我的祖母時常閱讀佛教經典。　　My grandmother often reads Buddhist scriptures.

那家人每週日都會去望彌撒。　　The family goes to mass every Sunday.

你週三也會去做禮拜嗎？　　　　Do you attend the service on Wednesdays as well?

我在10年前受洗為天主教徒。　　I was baptized a Catholic 10 years ago.

首爾有間清真寺。　　　　　　　There is a mosque in Seoul.

cross
十字架

pray 禱告
prayer 禱告

preach
宣教

hymn
聖詩、讚美詩

the Pope
教皇

cardinal
樞機主教

priest
神父、司鐸

nun
修女

minister
牧師

(Buddhist) monk
僧侶、師父
Buddhist nun 尼姑

rabbi
拉比
（猶太教的智者）

imam
（伊斯蘭教）伊瑪目

SENTENCES TO USE

我媽媽每天早上和傍晚都會禱告。	My mom prays every morning and evening.
我記得我小時候學過的一些聖詩。	I remember a few of the hymns I learned as a child.
教皇是全世界天主教堂的領袖。	The Pope is the head of the Catholic Church around the world.
韓國首位樞機主教是已故的金壽煥樞機。	The first cardinal in Korea is the late Cardinal Kim Soo-hwan.
我的叔叔是天主教神父。	My uncle is a Catholic priest.
韓國的僧侶不能結婚。	Korean Buddhist monks cannot get married.

Nowadays, most people read newspaper articles on the Internet.

There are a lot of people
doing personal broadcasting
these days.

CHAPTER

13

交通與駕駛

Traffic & Driving

交通相關

drive a car / truck / van
駕駛汽車 / 卡車 / 貨車

**take a bus / taxi
/ train / subway /
tram / boat / ship
/ ferry**
搭乘公車 / 計程車 /
火車 / 地鐵 / 電車 /
小船 / 大船 / 渡輪

**ride a bicycle[bike] /
motorcycle[motorbike] /
scooter / moped / horse**
騎腳踏車 / 機車 / 小型機車 /
輕型機踏車 / 馬

get on / **off a bus** 上 / 下公車
get in / **out of a car** / **taxi** 上 / 下汽車 / 計程車
catch a train / **bus** 搭火車 / 公車
miss a train / **bus** 錯過火車 / 公車
give someone a ride 載某人一程
hitchhike 搭便車

SENTENCES TO USE

我今天搭地鐵去市區。 — I took the subway to go downtown today.

一位提著包袱的年老女士艱難地上了公車。 — An old lady with a bundle got on the bus with difficulty.

我差點錯過公車。 — I almost missed the train.

我朋友載我回家。 — My friend gave me a ride home.

英文道路標誌
STOP：停止
DEAD END：此路不通
ONE WAY：單向道
DO NOT ENTER：禁止進入
YIELD, GIVE WAY：車輛先行

passenger
乘客

driver
駕駛

pedestrian
行人

road〔traffic〕sign
道路交通號誌

traffic light〔signal〕 紅綠燈
（**red light** 紅燈
green light 綠燈
yellow light 黃燈）

bus stop
公車站

taxi stand
計程車站

train station 火車站
platform 月臺

ticket office
售票處

**get through the ticket
gate〔ticket barrier〕**
通過票閘門

SENTENCES TO USE

行人應優先於車輛。	Pedestrians should be given priority over vehicles.
有時候交通號誌很難懂。	Sometimes it's hard to understand the road signs.
有一些車不遵守紅綠燈。	There are a few cars that don't observe the traffic signal.
醫院前方有一個計程車站。	There's a taxi stand in front of the hospital.
火車剛駛離月臺。	The train has just left the platform.
你通過票閘門後就會看到便利商店。	You'll see the convenience store as soon as you get through the ticket gate.

2 開車

fasten[wear] a seat belt
繫安全帶

go straight
直行

turn right / left
右轉 / 左轉

change lanes
變換車道

park 停車
parking lot 停車場

speed up, accelerate 加速
slow down 減速
brake 踩剎車
turn on a turn signal, put a turn signal on 打開方向燈
pick someone up 載某人
drop someone off 讓某人下車
observe / **neglect** / **violate the traffic signal** 遵守 / 無視 / 違反紅綠燈
honk one's horn 按喇叭

SENTENCES TO USE

現在車裡每個人都要繫安全帶。	Now we need to fasten seat belts on every seat of the vehicle.
如果你開車，就不能去沒有停車場的地方。	If you drive, you won't be able to go to places without a parking lot.
你下坡時應該減速。	You should slow down when you're going downhill.
你不應該立即踩剎車。	You shouldn't suddenly brake.
有些車沒有打開方向燈就變換車道。	There are cars that change lanes without turning on the turn signals.
不需要按喇叭的時候按喇叭是不可取的。	It's not desirable to honk your horn when it's not necessary.

have a car accident〔crash〕 出車禍　**break down** 故障　**have a flat tire** 輪胎沒氣　**tow a car** 拖吊

have〔get〕the car checked / repaired 檢查 / 修理汽車

car service center 汽車服務中心
auto〔car〕repair shop 汽車維修站
mechanic 維修技師

gas station 加油站
put gas in a car 加油
fill a car with gas, gas up 加滿油
（**gasoline** 汽油, **diesel** 柴油）

EV charging station
（**electric vehicle charging station**）
電動車充電站

charge an electric car
給電動車充電

SENTENCES TO USE

你開始開車之後有出過車禍嗎？　Haven't you ever had a car accident since you started driving?

我的車子故障，花很多錢去維修。　My car broke down and it cost me a lot to have it repaired.

我給汽車維修中心檢查我的車。　I had my car checked at the car service center.

最近的加油站在哪裡？　Where is the nearest gas station?

我們出發前加個油吧。　Let's put gas in the car before we hit the road.

附近有電動車充電站嗎？　Is there an electric vehicle charging station nearby?

wash a car 洗車
car wash 洗車場

go through an automatic car wash
通過自動洗車機

speed limit 限速

speed camera
測速照相機

get a speeding / parking ticket
被開超速 / 違停罰單

be congested 塞車
be stuck in a traffic jam
塞在路上

centerline 中線
crosswalk 斑馬線

get one's driver's license
取得駕照

used car 二手車
take out car insurance 保汽車險

SENTENCES TO USE

我在加油站加油，然後將車子開去自動洗車。	I put the gas in at the gas station and went through an automatic car wash.
高速公路速限是每小時110公里。	The speed limit on the highway is 110 kilometers per hour.
我光這個月就收到兩張違停罰單。	I got two parking tickets this month alone.
路上很塞。事實上那條路總是在塞車。	The road was very congested. In fact, there is always a heavy traffic jam on that road.
你幾歲取得駕照？	At what age did you get your driver's license?
我買二手車需要注意些什麼？	What should I be careful about when I buy a used car?

103

汽車構造: 外部

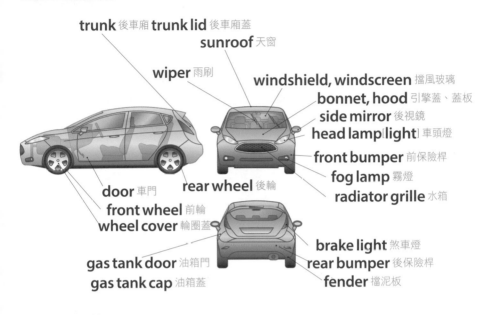

trunk 後車廂 trunk lid 後車廂蓋
sunroof 天窗
wiper 雨刷
windshield, windscreen 擋風玻璃
bonnet, hood 引擎蓋、蓋板
side mirror 後視鏡
head lamp[light] 車頭燈
front bumper 前保險桿
fog lamp 霧燈
radiator grille 水箱
door 車門
rear wheel 後輪
front wheel 前輪
wheel cover 輪圈蓋
brake light 煞車燈
rear bumper 後保險桿
gas tank door 油箱門
gas tank cap 油箱蓋
fender 擋泥板

汽車構造：內部

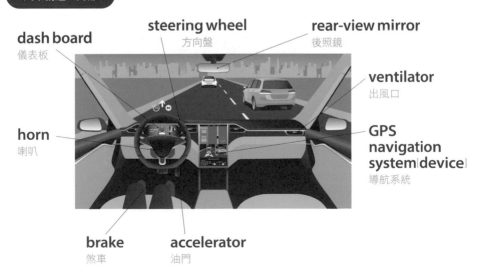

dash board
儀表板

steering wheel
方向盤

rear-view mirror
後照鏡

ventilator
出風口

horn
喇叭

GPS
navigation
system[device]
導航系統

brake
煞車

accelerator
油門

direction 方向
signpost 路標
road map 道路地圖
compass 指南針、羅盤
northeast 東北方
northwest 西北方
southeast 東南方
southwest 西南方
street 街道 (**st.**)
avenue 大街 (**ave.**)
boulevard 大道 (**blvd.**)
road （車輛行駛的）道路

north 北方
N
west 西方 **W** **E east** 東方
S
south 南方

SENTENCES TO USE

近來因為有導航，幾乎沒有人帶地圖找路了。

Nowadays, few people carry road maps because there are GPS navigation systems.

世宗市在大田廣域市的西北方。

Sejong City is in the northwest of Daejeon Metropolitan City.

boulevard, street, avenue, road
• boulevard：兩側有行道樹的寬的道路，通常有分隔島。
• street：兩側有建築物的道路。通常是東西向，和 avenue 垂直。
• avenue：兩側有建築物的道路。通常是南北向，和 street 垂直。
• road：車輛行駛的道路。

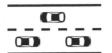

intersection, junction, crossroads 十字路口	highway, freeway, expressway 高速公路	one-way street 單向道	turn right / left 右轉 / 左轉

shoulder 路肩
sidewalk, pavement, footpath 人行道
go straight (**ahead**) 直行、直走
go past 經過～
stop at / **in front of** 在～停下
take the first / **second right** / **left** 第一個 / 第二個路口右轉 / 左轉
read a map 看地圖
ask the way (**to** 到～) 問路 / **ask for directions** 問路

SENTENCES TO USE

在十字路口右轉。	Turn right at the intersection.
在高速公路不能減速。	You can't drive slow on the highway.
直走200公尺後左轉。	Go straight for about 200 meters and then turn left.
行駛在路肩上很危險。	It's dangerous to drive on the shoulder.
經過郵局後在地鐵站停下。	Go past the post office and stop at the subway station.
如果不知道的話就問路。	Ask people the way if you don't know.

CHAPTER

14

手機、網路、社群媒體

Smartphone, Internet, Social Media

手機

unlock the smartphone
解鎖手機

text message
簡訊

text
傳簡訊

messaging[texting] app
即時通訊應用程式

---

slide to unlock, unlock the phone by sliding it to the side
滑動解鎖手機

enter a password / pattern to unlock the phone
輸入密碼 / 圖形解鎖手機

make a (phone) call 打電話
answer[get] a (phone) call, answer the phone 接電話
make[do] a video call 打視訊電話
use one's smartphone to access the Internet[to get online]
用手機上網

SENTENCES TO USE

她好像整天都在傳簡訊。	She seems to be texting all day.
韓國最流行的即時通訊應用程式是 Kakao Talk。	The most popular messaging app in Korea is Kakao Talk.
我輸入圖形解鎖手機。	I enter a pattern to unlock my smartphone.
她常常不接電話。	She often doesn't answer the phone.
他常常和他的小女兒通視訊電話。	He often makes video calls with his young daughter.
現在有很多人用智慧型手機上網。	Nowadays, many people use their smartphones to access the Internet.

use an application[app] 使用應用程式
download an application[app]
下載應用程式

install an application[app]
安裝應用程式

update an application[app]
更新應用程式

a battery runs out
電池沒電

(high-speed) (battery) charger
（快速）電池充電器

portable charger 行動電源
home screen 主畫面
lock screen 上鎖畫面

charge a phone
手機充電

SENTENCES TO USE

你下載那個廣播應用程式了嗎？	Did you install that radio app?
有5個應用程式需更新。	There are 5 apps that need to be updated.
我手機沒電，充個電再打給你。	The battery has run out so I'm going to charge it and call you again.
用快充幫智慧型手機充電比較好。	It's good to charge your smartphone with a high-speed charger.
智慧型手機很快沒電，所以我需要帶行動電源。	The smartphone battery runs out quickly, so I have to carry around a portable charger.
我把我的狗的照片設為手機主畫面。	I put a picture of my dog on my smartphone home screen.

網路、電子郵件

 網路

access a website
進入網站

surf[browse] the Internet
上網

****

enter one's User ID and password
輸入帳號密碼

bookmark a website[page]
將網頁加入書籤
bookmark 書籤

shop online
在線上購物
Internet[online] shopping
網路購物

click
點擊

search[look] for information on a portal site 在入口網站搜尋資訊
register[subscribe to] a website 加入網站會員
sign in[log in to] a website 登入網站
sign out of[log out of] a website 登出網站
copy 複製
paste 貼上

SENTENCES TO USE

我覺得我每天大約上網1小時。	I think I spend about an hour a day surfing the Internet.
請輸入帳號及密碼登入。	Please enter your User ID and password to sign in.
我將那個網站加入書籤。	I bookmarked that website.
我常常網購。	I shop online often.
最近大家都在入口網站找資料、看新聞。	These days, people look for information and watch the news on portal sites.
你可以複製貼上這句。	You can copy and paste the sentence.

sender 寄件人

recipient 收件人

subject 主旨

電子郵件

inbox 收件匣

outbox, sent email 寄件備份

drafts 草稿

spam[junk] email 垃圾信件

trash, deleted items 垃圾桶

body 本文

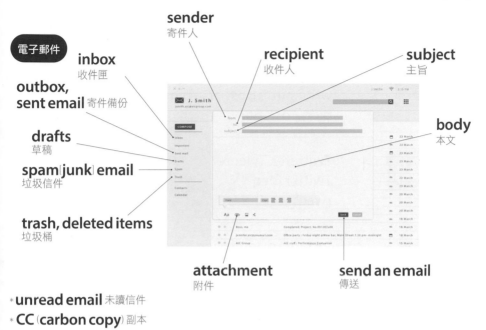

attachment 附件

send an email 傳送

* **unread email** 未讀信件
* **CC (carbon copy)** 副本

---

create an email account 建立電子信箱
log on[in] to one's email account 登入電子信箱
write an email 寫電子郵件
reply to an email 回電子郵件
forward an email 轉寄電子郵件

SENTENCES TO USE

我沒打主旨就寄信給她了。	I sent her an email without a subject.
我的收件匣有超過50封未讀信件。	I have over 50 unread mails in my inbox.
這封信請副本給經理。	Please send the email CCing the manager.
我建了一個新的電子郵件帳號。	I've created a new email account.
我有超過10封電子郵件要回。	I have over 10 emails to reply to.
請轉寄這封信給我。	Please forward the email to me.

blog 部落格、寫部落格
blogger 部落客
write[put] a post on a blog 寫部落格文章
blog post, post 部落格文章

Twitterer, Tweeter 推特用戶
Twitter feed 推特動態消息
tweet 推文

Instagram feed Instagram 動態消息
Instagrammer 使用 Instagram 的人
Instagrammable 值得上傳 Instagram 的

follow somebody on Twitter / Instagram 在推特 / Instagram 上追蹤某人
follower 追蹤者 / **following** 追蹤中

SENTENCES TO USE

我很久沒發部落格文章了。	It's been a while since I wrote a post on my blog.
看這則推文。	Look at this tweet.
我看他的 Instagram 動態消息看到忘了時間。	I've lost track of time watching his Instagram feed.
這是首爾最值得拍照上傳 Instagram 的十個景點之一。	It is one of the 10 most Instagrammable spots in Seoul.
我在推特上追蹤那位作家。	I followed the writer on Twitter.
那位歌手有超過一百萬人追蹤。	The singer has over a million followers.

have a Facebook account 有臉書帳號
join Facebook 加入臉書
write[put] a post on Facebook 在臉書上貼文

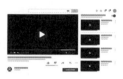

YouTube creator, YouTuber YouTube 創作者
open a YouTube channel 建立 YouTube 頻道
upload[post] a video on YouTube 上傳 YouTube 影片
subscribe to a YouTube channel 訂閱 YouTube 頻道
watch[view] a YouTube video 觀看 YouTube 影片

press "Like"
按讚

write a comment
留言

block somebody 封鎖某人
troll 惡意留言、酸民

SENTENCES TO USE

我有臉書帳號，但我很少用。	I have a Facebook account, but I rarely use it.
我訂閱一個擁有22隻貓的人的 YouTube 頻道。	I'm subscribing to the YouTube channel of a person who has 22 cats.
睡覺前看一些YouTube 影片是我的習慣。	It's my habit to watch some YouTube videos before going to bed.
他按讚我的貼文。	He pressed "Like" on my post.
我很少留言。	I hardly write comments.
那個男子團體提告酸民們。	The boy band sued trolls.

CHAPTER
15

教育

Education

教育相關

kindergarten
幼稚園

elementary school
國小

middle school
國中

high school
高中

college
學院（只到學士）、分院

university
大學

semester 學期
graduate school 研究所
academy 補習班

coeducational, coed 男女同校的
major 主修、主修～（**major in** ~）
cram school 升學補習班

SENTENCES TO USE

當我還小時，只有一些小孩會上幼稚園。

When I was a kid, only a few children went to kindergarten.

在2019年，韓國普通高中的學生上大學的比率是76.5%。

In 2019, the ratio of Korean general high school students going to college was 76.5 percent.

韓國的第二學期於8月開始。

In Korea, the second semester starts in August.

我的高中是男女混校。

My high school was coeducational.

我大學主修心理學。

I majored in psychology when in university.

很多中學生去上英文和數學的補習班。

Many middle school students attend English and math academies.

lecture 課
lecture room 課堂教室

textbook
教科書

diploma
畢業證書、文憑

library
圖書館

laboratory
實驗室、研究室

dormitory
宿舍

credit 學分
essay 課堂論文、課堂報告
midterm exam 期中考

degree 學位
thesis 學位論文
final exam 期末考

SENTENCES TO USE

我需要大學文憑才能申請。	I need a university diploma to apply for it.
那個系的學生整晚都在實驗室實驗和研究。	The students of the department experiment and study until late at night in the laboratory.
我希望我讀大學時選擇住宿。	I hoped I'd live in a dormitory when I'd go to college.
你這學期修幾學分？	How many credits are you taking this semester?
我本週忙於寫報告。	I've been busy writing an essay for the weekend.
我們下週要期末考。	Next week, we'll take the final exam.

professor
教授

instructor
講師、（特殊技術或運動）教練

graduate
畢業生

lifelong learning 終身學習
online learning 線上學習

freshman（高中、大學）新生、大一
sophomore 高二、大二
junior 大三
senior 高三、大學年級最高者
undergraduate 大學生
bachelor's degree 學士學位
master's degree 碩士學位
doctor's degree, doctorate, Ph. D. 博士學位

SENTENCES TO USE

你不知道終身學習嗎？你在任何年紀都可以學習。
Don't you know the word lifelong learning? You can learn at any age.

我在大二時學習英國文學史。
I learned the history of English literature in my sophomore year.

她是大學生，她男友是研究生。
She is an undergraduate and her boyfriend is a graduate school student.

你需要有博士學位才可以被聘為教授。
You need a doctor's degree to be hired as a professor.

美國、加拿大、韓國等地的大學教授體制
lecturer 講師 ≒ instructor 老師 > assistant professor 助理教授 > associate professor 副教授 > professor 教授、正教授 (full professor)

attend a class
出席課堂

**take〔sit〕
an exam〔a test〕**
考試

**pass / fail
an exam**
通過 / 未通過考試

graduate from
畢業於 ～

get a degree
取得學位

---

enter 入學
enroll in 選課
take〔listen to〕a course〔class〕 上課、聽課
earn credits 取得學分
get an A 獲得 A / **get a good grade** 得到好成績
apply for / get a scholarship 申請 / 獲得獎學金
take a year off〔from school〕休學1年

SENTENCES TO USE

我本週每天都有考試。 　　I'm taking tests every day this week.

我本學期選修西洋哲學史。 　I enrolled in Western philosophy class this semester.

我每週都要上詩的課程。 　　I'm taking a poetry class every week.

你這學習要修20學分才可以畢業。 You need to earn 20 credits this semester to graduate.

在大學的時候，除了學費自己付，我一直都獲得獎學金。 In college, I kept getting scholarships except for the admission fee.

我大學時休學1年。 　　　　I took a year off from college.

UNIT 1

學科、主修

國中、高中
art 美術
biology 生物
chemistry 化學
English 英文
ethics 道德、倫理
geography 地理
math, mathematics 數學
music 音樂
PE(**physical education**)體育
physics 物理
science 自然科學
second foreign language 第二外語
social studies 社會
world history 世界史

大學
aesthetics 美學
applied art 應用美術
architecture 建築學
astronomy 天文學
biology 生物學
business studies, business administration 經營學
ceramics 陶瓷工藝
chemical engineering 化學工程學
chemistry 化學
communication 傳播學
composition 作曲
dentistry 牙醫學
diplomatic science 外交學
drama 戲劇
early childhood education 幼教

economics 經濟學
education 教育學
electronic engineering 電子工程學
English education 英語教育
English language and literature 英國語言與文學
fashion design 時尚設計
geography 地理學
geology 地質學
history 歷史
industrial design 工業設計
industrial engineering 工業工程學
international relations 國際關係
international trade 國際貿易學
journalism and broadcasting 新聞傳播學
Korean literature 韓國文學
law 法學
math, mathematics 數學
mechanical engineering 機械工程學
media and communication 媒體傳播學
medicine 醫學
microbiology 微生物學
nursing science 護理學
oriental medicine 中醫
oriental painting 東洋畫
painting 繪畫
philosophy 哲學
physics 物理學
political science 政治學
psychology 心理學
sculpture 雕塑
sociology 社會學
veterinary medicine 獸醫學
visual communication design 視覺傳達設計

UNIT 2 外語

speak	practice	be fluent in	speak ~ fluently
說（語言）	練習（語言）	（語言）流利	～ 說得很流利

go to an English academy(institute)	learn / practice English conversation	bilingual
上英文補習班	學習 / 練習英語會話	說雙語的

~ **is poor** 不會（語言）
be good / poor at 會 / 不會（語言）
get rusty 生疏
native speaker 母語者
speaking / listening / reading / writing skills 口說 / 聽力 / 閱讀 / 寫作技巧

SENTENCES TO USE

你會說中文嗎？	Can you speak Chinese?
他的英文和德文流利。	He is fluent in English and German.
我在補習班學日語會話。	I learned Japanese conversation at the academy.
不好意思，我的英文不好。	I'm sorry my English is poor.
她的英文說得像母語人士一樣。	She speaks English like a native speaker.
我要怎麼提升英文寫作技巧？	How can I improve my English writing skills?

language barrier
語言障礙

vocabulary
單字

grammar
文法

translate 翻譯
translation 翻譯
translator 譯者

interpret 口譯
interpretation 口譯

interpreter 口譯員
simultaneous interpreter
同步口譯

accent 口音
intonation 語調
pronunciation 發音（**pronounce** 發音）

SENTENCES TO USE

她知道很多英文單字。	She has a large vocabulary of English.
我可以用英文溝通，但是我文法很弱。	I can communicate in English, but my English grammar is weak.
將《寄生上流》的韓文台詞翻譯成英文的達西帕奎特是一位電影評論家。	Darcy Paquet, who translated the lines of *Parasite* into English, is a film critic.
我的小孩的夢想是成為一位同步口譯員。	My child's dream is to become a simultaneous interpreter.
他的英文有印度口音。	He speaks English with an Indian accent.
那個單字的發音很難。	It's hard to pronounce that word.

CHAPTER

16

世界與環境

World & Environment

世界、地球

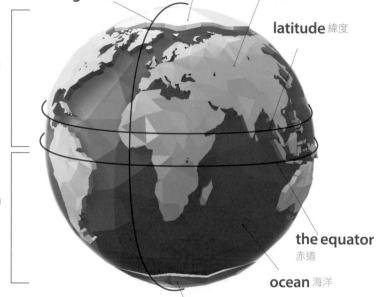

the North Pole 北極 / the Arctic 北極、北極區
the Arctic Circle 北極圈
longitude 經度
continent 大陸
latitude 緯度
the Northern Hemisphere 北半球
the Southern Hemisphere 南半球
the equator 赤道
ocean 海洋
the South Pole 南極 / the Antarctic 南極、南極區
the Antarctic Circle 南極圈 / Antarctica 南極大陸
(the) Earth, (the) planet earth 地球

SENTENCES TO USE

地球是太陽系的行星之一。	The Earth is a planet in the solar system.
第一位抵達北極的人是美國探險家羅伯特佩里。	The first person to reach the North Pole was American explorer Robert Peary.
冰島就位於北極圈的南方。	Iceland is located just south of the Arctic Circle.
厄瓜多的命名是因為它位於赤道。	Ecuador got such a name because it lies on the equator.
獨島（日本稱作竹島）位於北緯37.14度，東經131.5度。	Dokdo is located at 37.14 degrees north latitude and 131.5 degrees east longitude.
南半球的人於夏季慶祝聖誕節。	They celebrate Christmas during the summer in the Southern Hemisphere.

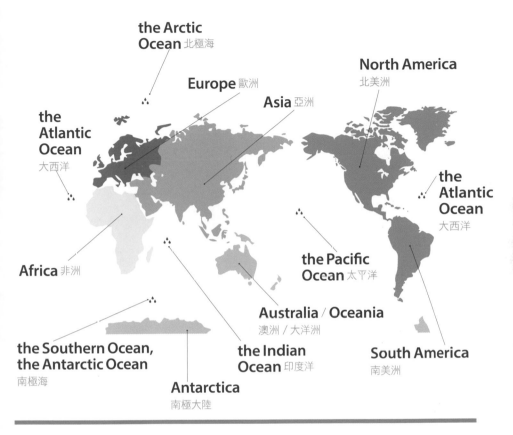

the Arctic
Ocean 北極海

North America
北美洲

Europe 歐洲

Asia 亞洲

the
Atlantic
Ocean
大西洋

the
Atlantic
Ocean
大西洋

Africa 非洲

the Pacific
Ocean 太平洋

the Southern Ocean,
the Antarctic Ocean
南極海

Australia / Oceania
澳洲 / 大洋洲

the Indian
Ocean 印度洋

South America
南美洲

Antarctica
南極大陸

SENTENCES TO USE

最大的大陸是亞洲,第二大
是非洲。

The largest continent is Asia and the second largest is
Africa.

地球上最大的海洋是太平洋。

The largest ocean on Earth is the Pacific Ocean.

南極海指的是環繞南極大陸
的海洋。

The Antarctic Ocean refers to the ocean surrounding
Antarctica.

the tropics, tropical region 熱帶
（≒ **low latitudes** 低緯度區）

**the subtropics,
subtropical region** 亞熱帶

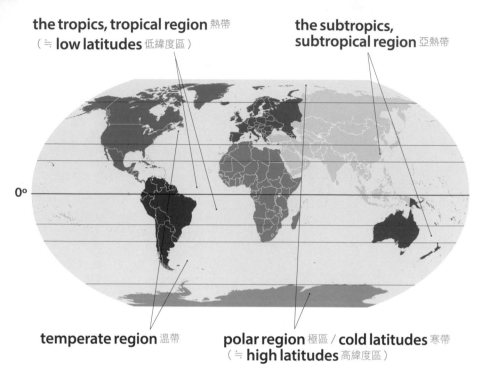

0°

temperate region 溫帶

polar region 極區 / **cold latitudes** 寒帶
（≒ **high latitudes** 高緯度區）

SENTENCES TO USE

印度跨越了亞熱帶及熱帶區。 India spans from a subtropical region to
a tropical region.

極區是環繞北極和南極的區域。 The polar regions are the regions that surround the
North Pole and South Pole.

113

Asian
亞洲人

North American
北美洲人

Latin American
拉丁美洲人

African 非洲人
African American
非裔美國人

European
歐洲人

Mongoloid
黃種人（蒙古人種）

white person, Caucasian
白人

black person
黑人

✦ **person of color** 非白人

SENTENCES TO USE

我住的青年旅館裡，有5位亞洲人、4位歐洲人和3位拉丁美洲人。

There were five Asians, four Europeans and three Latin Americans in the youth hostel where I stayed.

美國黑人現在被稱作非裔美國人。

Black Americans are now called African-Americans.

因紐特人屬於黃種人。

Inuits are members of the Mongoloid race.

person of color
黃種人或黑人等有色人種，過去被稱作 a colored person，但因為有歧視和不平等的意味，現在稱作 a person of color。

2 地形、地理

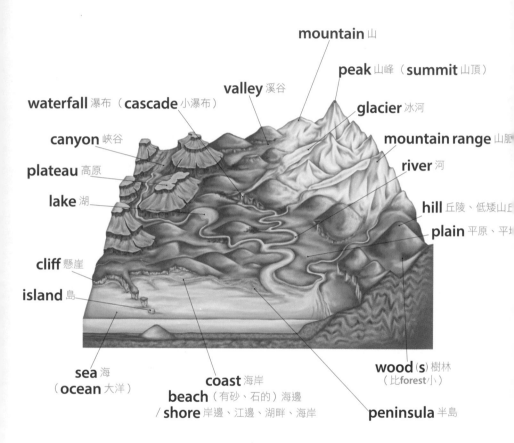

mountain 山

peak 山峰（summit 山頂）

valley 溪谷

waterfall 瀑布（cascade 小瀑布）

glacier 冰河

canyon 峽谷

mountain range 山脈

plateau 高原

river 河

lake 湖

hill 丘陵、低矮山丘

plain 平原、平地

cliff 懸崖

island 島

wood (s) 樹林
（比forest小）

sea 海
（ocean 大洋）

coast 海岸
beach（有砂、石的）海邊
/ shore 岸邊、江邊、湖畔、海岸

peninsula 半島

SENTENCES TO USE

世界上最有名的峽谷一定是大峽谷。 — The most famous canyon in the world must be the Grand Canyon.

當我年紀越大，比起海更喜歡山。 — As I get older, I like mountains better than the sea.

那個山脈位於中部和南部的分界。 — The mountain range borders the central and southern regions.

因為地球暖化，每年有大量冰河正融化中。 — Due to global warming, lots of glaciers are melting away each year.

我家後面有一座小山。 — There is a hill behind my house.

新加坡位於馬來半島南端。 — Singapore is located at the southern tip of the Malay Peninsula.

里約熱內盧的科帕卡巴納海灘是世界上最有名的海灘之一。 — Copacabana Beach in Rio de Janeiro is one of the world's most famous beaches.

退潮時，島和陸地相連，所以你可以直接走過去。 — During the low tide, the island is connected to the land and you can walk there.

世界最大最高的高原是青藏高原，常常被稱作世界屋脊。 — The largest and highest plateau in the world is the Tibetan Plateau, often called the roof of the world.

beach, coast, shore
• beach：人們會去做水上活動、日光浴的有砂、石的海邊
• coast：海岸或海洋附近的陸地
• shore：江、湖、海的沿岸

volcano 火山	**cave** 洞穴	**desert** 沙漠	**dune** 沙丘

forest 森林

rain forest 雨林

jungle 叢林

swamp 沼澤

iceberg 冰山

stream 溪流

pond 池塘

grassland, meadow, pasture 草地、草原

field 田野

farmland 田地

countryside 鄉下

wave 海浪、波浪

horizon 地平線

rising tide, high tide, flood tide 漲潮

low tide 退潮

SENTENCES TO USE

白頭山是休火山，意思是隨時可能爆發。

Mount Baekdu is a dormant volcano. It means it can explode anytime.

世界上最大的熱沙漠是非洲的撒哈拉沙漠。

The largest hot desert in the world is the Sahara in Africa.

亞馬遜雨林是世界上最大的熱帶雨林。

The Amazon rainforest is the largest tropical rainforest in the world.

羊群正在草原上吃草。

A flock of sheep is grazing in the meadow.

因為幾乎無風，所以海浪平靜。

Since there's not much wind, the waves are calm.

遠處的地平線上掛著太陽。

There's the sun on the horizon far away.

休火山、死火山
- dormant volcano 休火山：dormant 是「休息中的、睡的」之意
- extinct volcano 死火山：extinct 是「停止活動、熄火、滅絕」之意。

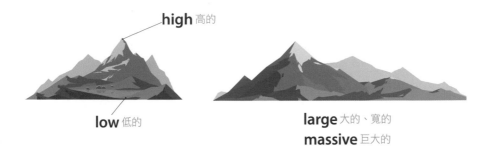

high 高的

low 低的

large 大的、寬的
massive 巨大的

wide 寬的　　**narrow** 窄的

shallow
淺的

deep
深的

steep 陡峭的、傾斜的
sharp 陡峭的、險峻的

vast, extensive 廣闊的、廣大的

SENTENCES TO USE

裏海是世界上最大的湖。	The Caspian Sea is the largest lake in the world.
澳洲中部的烏魯魯是一塊巨大的岩石。	Uluru, in central Australia, is a massive rock.
亞馬遜河是世界上最大的河嗎？	Is the Amazon River the widest river in the world?
孩子們正在淺的溪流中嬉戲。	The children are playing in a shallow stream.
他正靠著一條繩子爬上陡峭的岩石。	He was climbing up a steep rock with a rope.
這家人擁有一塊廣闊的地。	The family owned a vast tract of land.

nature 自然（**Mother Nature** 大自然）   **ecosystem** 生態系
creature 生物、生命體   **organism** 有機體、生物
microorganism 微生物   **plant** 植物   **animal** 動物

動物

mammal
哺乳類

bird
鳥類

amphibian
兩棲類

reptile
爬蟲類

fish
魚類

insect, bug
昆蟲、蟲子

SENTENCES TO USE

這樣做是在破壞生態系的秩序。

It is to destroy the order of the ecosystem.

目前知道第一位研究微生物的人是17世紀的雷文霍克。

The first person to study microorganisms is known as Anton van Leeuwenhoek in the 17th century.

獅子與老虎是夜行性動物。

Lions and tigers are nocturnal animals.

鯨魚生活在海裡，但牠們是哺乳類。

Whales live in the sea, but they are mammals.

青蛙是兩棲類還是爬蟲類？

Are frogs amphibians or reptiles?

昆蟲佔了地球上動物的90%以上。

Insects make up more than 90 percent of animals on Earth.

oxygen
氧

hydrogen
氫

carbon
碳

nitrogen
氮

carbon dioxide
(CO_2)
二氧化碳

ozone layer
臭氧層

atmosphere
大氣

EARTH

ultraviolet rays
[light]
紫外線

infrared rays[light]
紅外線

gas
氣體

liquid
液體

solid
固體

rock
岩石、石頭、石子

stone
石、石子

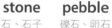
pebble
礫石、卵石

* **sand** 沙
* **mud** 泥土

* **soil** 土、土壤
* **mineral** 礦物

SENTENCES TO USE

水由氫和氧組成。 — Water is composed of hydrogen and oxygen.

二氧化碳被認為是溫室效應的主因。 — Carbon dioxide is considered the main cause of the greenhouse effect.

應該避免臭氧層被破壞。 — The ozone layer should be prevented from being destroyed.

地球大氣的99%是氮和氧。 — Nitrogen and oxygen make up 99 percent of the Earth's atmosphere.

紫外線是皮膚的敵人。 — Ultraviolet rays are the enemy of the skin.

水以氣體、液體、固體的狀態存在。 — Water exists in gas, liquid, and solid states.

環境問題

environmental protection 環境保護
environmental problem 環境問題
environmental pollution 環境污染
environmentalist, environmental activist 環保運動人士

global warming 地球暖化
greenhouse gas 溫室氣體
greenhouse effect 溫室效應

**environment-friendly,
eco-friendly**
環保的

climate change
氣候變遷

fossil fuel
化石燃料

SENTENCES TO USE

環境污染對所有人來說都是嚴重的問題。	Environmental pollution is a serious problem for all mankind.
美國前副總統高爾是位環保運動人士。	Former U.S. Vice President Al Gore is an environmentalist.
因為環境破壞造成地球平均溫度上升，就是地球暖化。	Global warming is the rise of the average global temperature due to environmental destruction.
破壞大氣並導致溫室效應的氣體，被稱作溫室氣體。	Gases that pollute the atmosphere and cause a greenhouse effect are called greenhouse gases.
我們必須思考環保的生活方式。	We have to think about the eco-friendly way of life.
諸如煤、石油、天然氣等化石燃料的使用導致空氣污染。	The use of fossil fuels such as coal, oil and natural gas has caused air pollution.

green energy 綠色能源
renewable energy 可再生能源
alternative energy 替代能源

solar energy, solar power 太陽能
solar panel 太陽能光電板
solar power generation 太陽能發電

wind power
風力

wind farm
風力發電廠

forest conservation
森林保護

forest destruction
森林破壞

recycle
回收

*geothermal energy** 地熱能

SENTENCES TO USE

我們需要發展和使用綠色能源來保護環境。

We need to develop and use green energy to protect the environment.

這個公寓有太陽能光電板。

The apartment has solar panels.

地熱能是利用地下水或地熱的能源。

Geothermal energy is energy using groundwater or underground heat.

green energy, **renewable energy**, **alternative energy**
這三個詞幾乎是同樣意思。都是指替代破壞環境的化石燃料，為親環境且可再生的能源。
代表性的有太陽光能、太陽熱能、風力、地熱能、水力、熱液能、海洋能（浪潮、波浪）、生物能源、氫能、燃料電池、煤液化、煤氣化等。

INDEX 索引

E

T

Z

etc.

Y

EZ TALK

圖解英語會話關鍵單字

作　　　者：徐寧助
譯　　　者：陳靖婷
責 任 編 輯：謝有容
裝 幀 設 計：初雨有限公司（ivy_design）
內 頁 排 版：初雨有限公司（ivy_design）
行 銷 企 劃：陳品萱

發 行 人：洪祺祥
副 總 經 理：洪偉傑
副 總 編 輯：曹仲堯
法 律 顧 問：建大法律事務所
財 務 顧 問：高威會計師事務所

出　　　版：日月文化出版股份有限公司
製　　　作：EZ叢書館
地　　　址：臺北市信義路三段151號8樓
電　　　話：(02) 2708-5509
傳　　　真：(02) 2708-6157
網　　　址：www.heliopolis.com.tw
郵 撥 帳 號：19716071日月文化出版股份有限公司

總 經 銷：聯合發行股份有限公司
電　　　話：(02) 2917-8022
傳　　　真：(02) 2915-7212

印　　　刷：中原造像股份有限公司
初　　　版：2023年1月
定　　　價：380元
I S B N：978-626-7238-06-6

圖解英語會話關鍵單字 / 徐寧助著；陳靖
譯. -- 初版. -- 臺北市：日月文化出版股份
限公司, 2023.01
320 面；14.7 x 21 公分. -- (EZ talk:)
譯自：영어 회화의 결정적 단어들
ISBN 978-626-7238-06-6（平裝）
1.CST: 英語 2.CST: 會話 3.CST: 詞彙
805.188　　　　　　　　　1110181